BLUE BOY 2: BONES

Garrett Leigh

Blue Boy 2: Bones

Copyright © May 2017 by Garrett Leigh

All rights reserved. No part of this book may be used or reproduced by any means without the written permission of Fox Love Press except in the case of brief quotation embodied in critical articles and reviews.

Cover Artist: Garrett Leigh @ Black Jazz Design
Published in the United Kingdom

This book is a work of fiction. While reference might be made to actual historical events or existing locations, the names, characters, places and incidents are either the product of the author's imagination or are used fictitiously, and any resemblance to actual persons, living or dead, business establishments, events, or locales is entirely coincidental.

DEDICATION

For those who've been with me from the start

CHAPTER ONE

Cam fought the silk ties restraining his wrists. The knots were loose, and his arms were strong. With enough effort he could be free in moments. Free to roll over and demand what he wanted. Free to do anything and be anywhere but here.

A soft puff of air washed over his spine, belying the firm hands on his hips. "Still."

The effect of the command was instant, calming Cam from the inside out. His heart beat like a racing freight train, but the desire to defy his binds evaporated.

He sucked in a shaky breath. Away from Jon Kellar, his lover of sorts, he resisted the submissive role he'd accidentally fallen into, but when they were together, it was easy to give in to the dark temptation of Jon's bed. Easy to fall back into a place where time stood still and there was nothing in the world but the carnal pleasure of someone else calling the shots.

"Spread your legs."

Cam obeyed and arched his back with a groan, craving the sensation of Jon's cock pressing inside him, even though he knew Jon would keep him hanging for hours yet.

At least, it often felt like hours. Jon Kellar was a master manipulator, and Cam knew he wouldn't give up his game of teasing temptation until Cam was begging…screaming for more.

Warm breath rushed over Cam's skin, and then the light brush of the feather Jon liked to skim over his cock. Cam shuddered, feeling the first strands of desperation deep in his belly.

Jon rubbed his hand over Cam's sweat-slicked back, kneading until he came to the curved muscle of Cam's ass. He slapped Cam with enough force to leave a pleasurable burn. "What do you want? Want me to fuck you?"

Cam moaned. It was too soon for him to lose his head, but *damn*, this shit felt good. Too good.

Jon chuckled and slapped Cam again, soothing the heated sting with the palm of his hand. "Maybe I'll rim you first. Would you like that?"

"Fuck yeah."

"Quiet."

The silence was long and excruciating. Cam trembled, and his thighs quivered with a need only Jon had ever provoked. Christ, Jon was the only man he'd ever bottomed for at all, let alone given over control of his body.

What the hell are you doing?

Some days, he didn't know, and others, he knew Jon had caught him at a weak time in his life and shown him how to lose himself in desire and sex until the rest of the world faded away. And then some days…fuck. Some days all he knew was a craving so deep his bones felt like they could combust into smoke and ash.

Jon trailed the tip of the feather down the crease of Cam's ass and moved lower, ghosting over his balls. On fire, Cam gritted his teeth and forced himself to stay still until he was finally rewarded by the sweeping touch of Jon's tongue.

He dropped his head to the mattress and widened his legs. He'd never been into rimming before he'd answered the ad in the back of the LGBT newsletter in his senior year at college. Fast-forward four years and he was a veteran porn star, and he couldn't get enough. Especially with Jon. Everything was better with Jon, in the bedroom at least.

Jon teased him with the tip of his tongue, alternating between light, gentle licks and toe-curling, stabbing thrusts. He kept his hands busy on Cam's body too, manipulating his tense, twitching muscles and rubbing his back. He grazed Cam's balls with his nails and pinched the insides of Cam's thighs.

He was everywhere, except where Cam wanted him most.

Cam jerked and tugged again at his binds, watching his aching cock drip on the smooth cotton sheets below him. "Jon…"

Jon chuckled and bit Cam's ass cheek. "Something you want?"

"You know what I want." Cam ground the words out through clenched teeth. They played this game all the time—the one where he ducked his head and begged…said please like a good boy—but Cam always fought it. Always gave Jon a reason to push him harder.

"Do I?" Jon took his hands from Cam's body. The rustling sheets and sudden gust of cool air told Cam he'd moved away. "Maybe I need reminding."

The click of the lube bottle opening drowned out the crackle of a condom wrapper. Cam tensed, knowing the blunt intrusion of Jon's cock wasn't too far away. "Fuck me."

"I can't hear you, Cam."

"*Fuck me*," Cam said louder. "Goddamn it."

"Hmm." Jon drizzled warming lube on Cam's ass and massaged it in with his thumb. "Maybe I should make you wait a little longer."

The tingle of the lube stung a moment before it seeped into Cam's skin and warmed him from the inside out. He squirmed, knowing exactly what Jon wanted, and hating himself for giving it up. "Please."

Jon stilled his devilish thumb. "I can't hear you."

Cam sucked in deep breaths, trying to calm the tremors rocking his body. His senses dulled and narrowed his perspective, leaving only anticipation and the aching throb of his cock. Somewhere in the back of his mind, he laughed. How did Jon do this? Narrow his universe to just the heady brew of desire?

"Focus." Jon slid a single finger into Cam, stretching him with practiced motions. The snap of latex pierced the air. "Say it again."

A low moan escaped Cam. "*Please.*"

Jon's finger disappeared, replaced by his condom-covered cock. Cam arched against the intrusion, feeling the dizzying burn of being filled sweep over him.

Jon steadied him, his hands almost soothing on Cam's overheated skin. "Relax. Don't fight what you need."

In Cam's mind, he tore the silk ties apart, ripped free, and pushed himself back onto Jon, chasing the bittersweet slam of their bodies, but in reality he held stone still, ready for whatever Jon would give him.

Jon slid into him, hard and fast. Cam gasped and for a moment longed for Jon to hold him closer to wrap his arms around Cam's waist and cover his body, but the feeling faded as the punishing beat of Jon's hips overcame coherent thought.

Cam gritted his teeth as Jon fucked him and took him to the brink of something mind-blowing, over and over, only to ease off each time before the punch line. Frustrated, Cam moaned and shuddered, making sounds only Jon had ever heard. The need to come became the only thing in his world. Sweat dripped from his body. His hair hung low in his face, and his cock throbbed so hard it *hurt*.

He groaned, long and loud, clenching his bound fists, desperate to grab on to something, anything. Even his own hair. *So good. So good.* "More…"

On cue, Jon slowed his thrusts to a dull roar and reached around, closing his fingers around Cam's dick. "Like this?"

The light touch was like a thunderbolt. Cam jerked, bucked, and growled, low and deep. "Shit, yeah."

Jon moved his hand in counterpoint with his hips. Once. Twice. Three times. "Come."

The command lit the fuse and triggered the climax Cam had held back for so long. He came hard, yelling his release and fighting the silk ties that bound him to the bed. "Fuck, fuck, *fuck*."

Behind him, Jon grunted and pulled out, the only sign of his own climax the sudden, warm spurt on Cam's back, before he untied Cam and rolled away.

Cam fell forward, exhausted, and collapsed into the sticky mess on the bed, watching in his peripheral vision as Jon got up and left the room. The bathroom door closed. The shower turned on, and he knew that was his cue to move too.

He slid off the bed, gathered the sheets, and dumped them into the hamper. His clothes littered the floor. He picked them up, feeling the way he always did after sex with Jon—sated, satisfied, and empty.

A little while later, Cam took his turn in the shower and drifted into Jon's minimalist living space to find him already seated behind his computer.

Jon didn't look up as he entered the room. That was typical too. Their evenings together followed a predictable routine—dinner, frustrating foreplay, mind-blowing sex, and then…nothing. Recently, the prefuck dinner had become an optional extra, though there was always a plentiful supply of Jon's expensive liquor.

Cam suppressed a sigh. They weren't dating, and he wasn't naive enough to believe he was the only Blue Boy model getting off in Jon's bed, but the silence stung.

He approached Jon from behind and put his hands on Jon's

shoulders, squeezing the wiry muscle he found there. Jon was fast approaching forty but still had the body of a much younger man. "What are you doing?"

"The schedule for next month."

Cam peered at the screen. "What am I doing?"

"Breaking in some newbies."

Cam let the sigh he'd been holding escape. Really? More massages and dull-as-rocks blowjobs from skittish rookies? That was another thing about fooling around with Jon. Jon still paid him the same, but it had been *months* since he'd shot a full sex scene. Months since he'd done anything more than lie back and get sucked off on-screen. "Can't I do something else?"

"Like what?"

"I don't know." Cam stared at the faces of his colleagues rolling across the screen. Kai, Jimmy, Sonny. The fresh face of a model he'd broken in six months ago flashed up. "What about Jack?"

"Jack's a top."

"So?"

Jon looked at Cam for the first time since making him come like a train, and his icy blue gaze hardened. "You want to bottom on-screen?"

"Sure. Why not?"

Jon shook his head. "It doesn't fit your brand."

"My brand?"

"You're the top everyone loves. The top that looks after his bottoms and gives them a good ride. Getting fucked will undermine that."

Cam raised an incredulous eyebrow. Jon had always been difficult to read, but his porn philosophy was goddamned bizarre. How could he brand Cam a top when he hadn't assigned Cam a hard-core scene in months? "You didn't say that about Levi. You all but forced him into it."

"And look what happened there. The scene was a bust, and I lost a lucrative model."

Cam knew there was far more to Levi's departure from Blue Boy, but he held his tongue. There was no love lost between his friend and his warped kind-of lover, and the less said about each of them in the other's company, the better. "You sound like you're losing your nerve."

"And you sound like you've got too much time on your hands. Trust me, when I get requests for you, it's not from people who want to see you get nailed. Stick to what you're good at."

Jon turned back to his work, the discussion closed. Cam took his dismissal and left.

CHAPTER TWO

Pop. Slam. Skid.

Cam maneuvered his skateboard along the sketchy park railing and popped out a lackadaisical laser flip. The landing wasn't great, but he stayed upright. Not bad for seven a.m. Though there was no one around, he grinned and gave the air a punch. Levi said Cam was too old to be boarding to work, that he should hang it up and get a car like the rest of the world. Cam called bullshit every damned time. He was twenty-five, not fifty, and even then they'd have to pry his board from his cold, dead hands.

It was a long skate to work, though. Forty-five minutes when the weather was good. An hour if he had to pick up and walk. Lucky for him, part of his journey took him along the deserted, early morning beachfront—his favorite place on earth. The sun in his eyes, the ocean breeze in his face, he'd yet to find a better way to start his day.

He skidded to a stop outside Beat Shak, the music store that made up his day job, just before eight. He was the first there, but that was typical. Early shifts suited him, and there weren't often any other takers. Good job too, as he doubted anyone else would be awake enough to deal with the washed-up visitor waiting on the bench outside.

Sonny.

Cam greeted him with open arms. Sonny walked right into them and placed a firm, platonic kiss on Cam's lips, tangling his fingers in Cam's riot of auburn hair.

"You're late today. I've been waiting ages."

Cam glanced at his watch. "It's not that late, Son. What time did you leave the club?"

"Dunno, dunno." Sonny bounced on the balls of his feet, still wired from his night, dancing on the podiums at Silver, the hippest gay club in town. "Just wanted to see your freakish morning smile."

Cam rewarded him with a wide grin, knowing his cheerful early morning habits bemused the hell out of night-owl Sonny. "Have you got classes today?"

Sonny danced into the shop behind him and took a seat at the digital-services counter that doubled as a juice bar. "At ten. No point going home."

Cam rolled his eyes. He didn't dig Sonny's habit of staying awake for days at a time, but who was he to judge? He'd said his piece once, and that was enough. He was Sonny's friend, not his mother, and it wasn't like Sonny was banging coke up his nose, though in some ways, Cam could've dealt with that…understood it, even if he wouldn't like it.

He threw an extra breakfast burrito in the microwave. Didn't want the hottest dancer in LA to starve, and though Cam could tell Levi had been feeding Sonny up, Sonny was pretty crappy at feeding himself. "Good night?"

Sonny hummed, still grooving to his own tune. "Yeah. The tips were good. Some dude tried to shove a twenty up my ass, though. I'm down for a lot of shit, but that wasn't cool. Security chucked him out."

"Was Jon there?"

"I didn't see him." Sonny shot him a waspish stare.

Cam averted his gaze. "How does Levi feel about you dancing up a storm for other dudes?"

"Never asked him."

"That's dangerous."

"Not really." Sonny rubbed his eyes. He looked weary, despite his incorrigible spirit. "He knew what he was getting into. Besides, he'd be the one fucking the whole studio if his mom hadn't died. He didn't give up porn for me."

Cam absorbed that. "Can't be easy, though. Sharing you. Has he ever asked you to cut back on your hard-core scenes?"

"No, and I don't think he ever would. What's with all the questions? You know Levi's cool. Something on your mind?"

Cam rummaged in the under-counter fridge for soda. "Just curious. You know how it is."

Sonny grinned. Their shared fascination with psychology was what had brought them together in the first place. Working for Jon was a devilish and fortuitous coincidence.

"Look at it this way," Sonny said. "Levi and I do shit together we don't do with anyone else. Have never done with anyone else. Maybe you should do that too. Find someone to share something special with. Separate your real sex life from the studio."

Cam opened the cash register. He'd be lying if he said he'd never wondered about Sonny and Levi's sex life. Sonny was kind of toppy for a bottom—demanding and dominant—and Levi liked to be in control. It was an interesting mix and one Cam had pondered a lot.

But Sonny's choice of words distracted him from any X-rated musings, and not in a good way. Sonny was always talking about *real* sex, like there was another world out there away from porn, a world Cam had forgotten about. "I wasn't talking about me."

"Because of Jon?"

Cam didn't answer. Sonny knew something had happened between him and Jon a few months ago, but Cam had yet to admit it was still going on. He wondered what Sonny would say if he knew how Cam submitted to Jon and how readily he let another man take control of his body.

You know exactly what he'd say.

The microwave pinged. Cam slid a nasty, boxed burrito Sonny's way. Sonny wrinkled his nose. Cam laughed, glad of the distraction. "You're spending way too much time with Momma Levi."

Sonny shrugged, unashamed. "The dude cooks and puts out. The perfect man, when he's not a grouch bag."

"Levi's always a grouch bag. It's part of his charm."

"I know." Sonny smiled, though Cam got the distinct impression it wasn't for him and instead for the private moment between Sonny and whatever image was floating through his kooky brain.

Cam didn't mind. He hadn't seen much of Levi since he'd severed his contract with Blue Boy, and he knew that was because Levi figured Cam was too close to Jon, but he saw Sonny all the time and could tell something special was building between him and Levi. Something Cam had never foreseen, even when his own flippant remark to Jon had pushed them together…

"Levi and Sonny? Interesting." Jon beckoned Sonny over and put the idea to him.

Sonny rolled his eyes. Most models treated Jon with a kind of reverence, but not Sonny. "No fucking way. I don't do jocks with cocks."

Cam spluttered into his drink. "Are you kidding? Dude, Levi's not like that. He's the warmest guy you'll ever meet. And he's smart too, smarter than all of us. Don't put him down."

Jon raised an eyebrow, but Cam ignored him. He was the wrong side of drunk to filter his words, and it annoyed the crap out of him when folk assumed big, brawny, huge-hearted Levi was as thick as his vital statistics.

Sonny stared at him with curious eyes. "Warm? He walks around like he's dead inside."

Cam sighed and tipped the last of his drink into his mouth. "If he ends up that way, it won't be his fault. That dude needs to be loved. Fuck, he deserves to be loved."

Cam had never expected Sonny to take his drunken rant so literally.

"Are you on the filming schedule tomorrow?"

Cam nodded through a bite of cheap, pasty burrito. "First up."

"Another handjob scene?" Sonny raised an eyebrow and picked at his breakfast. "You should just quit if that's all you're going to do. I'll see you right a few times a week. Levi wouldn't mind."

There was mirth in Sonny's words, but they struck a little close to home for Cam's liking. He finished his breakfast in silence and busied himself with his preopening checklist, hoping Sonny would get the hint.

Sonny didn't. "Why don't you come in on my scene with Luke? I can handle you both. It'll be fun, like old times."

A shiver of yearning ran through Cam. He used to shoot with Sonny all the time, more often than not carrying on long after they left the studio. He'd had Sonny every way he could think of, and it had always been fun. There were no romantic feelings between them, but their sexual chemistry was hot as hell when the context worked out.

His mind flashed unbidden to the last time he'd fucked Sonny, bent over the couch in his apartment. He pictured Sonny's perfect body writhing beneath him, shining with sweat and streaked with leftover body paint from a wild night at Silver.

Damn. The image in his head wasn't even Sonny. It was every guy he'd ever fucked. What the hell did that mean? Maybe Sonny was right and he *did* need to put himself out there again.

"Earth to Cam?"

"Huh?"

"Never mind." Sonny slid from his stool and came around the counter. He wrapped his arms around Cam's neck and pulled him down for another chaste kiss. "I might see you tomorrow if you're still at the studio. If not, call me, okay? Levi misses you, and you know he won't pick up the phone. He only calls me for the fuck-awesome phone sex."

Sonny spun away from Cam with a graceful twirl that belied his dirty wink. Cam said good-bye with an absent wave. He missed Levi too, and he knew better than to wait for the stubborn brute to come and find him. "Hey, Son?"

"Yeah?"

"Go home after class, okay? Get some sleep."

The rest of the day passed in a predictable haze. The store was a pleasant mix of the past and the ever-changing present, and Cam spent most of his day sorting stone-age vinyl on one side of the shop and helping the technologically inept get to grips with digital music on the other.

At lunchtime, he threw another plastic-wrapped roll of junk into the microwave on the juice bar.

"You're not going to eat that, are you?"

Cam glanced over his shoulder and met a set of the warmest brown eyes he'd ever seen. Darker brown than Sonny's hazel, they were flecked with gold and made the blond guy's grin like the early fall sun. "That's the plan."

The guy cast his gaze around the juice bar. "All this vitamin C and you choose that crap? Shame on you, man."

Cam shrugged. He'd heard it all before from his mom, when she was still around to notice, Levi, and just about every other weirdo who liked to pick their way through the grocery store, squeezing melons and prodding tomatoes. "It'll do me. Can I help you with something?"

"Aren't you on a break?" The guy gestured to the rotating microwave. "I can ask someone else."

"Nah." Cam came around the counter and held out his hand for the battered vinyl sleeve the guy was holding. "It'll keep. What do you need?"

The guy relinquished the sleeve. "I'm looking for this for my mom. She's had it since the seventies, but the record got broke when me and my bro were moving our bike shit around in the garage. I figure she won't be as pissed if I get a replacement before we tell her."

"Bike shit? Motorcycles?" Cam studied the record sleeve. The guy was starting to look familiar. Perhaps he knew Levi.

"BMX."

Something clicked in Cam's head. "Do you work at Tate's Bikes a few blocks away? I get board parts from there sometimes."

"That's my store." Hot Guy held out his hand. "Sasha Tate."

That explained the grungy board shorts, tanned forearms, and surfer-style hair. "Cam. Nice to meet you. I haven't been in for a while, but your place is pretty rad."

"Thanks. You should come by sometime after work. A bunch of us usually go hang at the Basin until sundown."

The Basin was the colloquial name for the only park in Venice Beach where skateboarders and BMXers rode together in harmony. Every other park in town was strictly one or the other, and *no one* liked the bladers. Cam hadn't been down there in a while, though. Most days life seemed to get in the way. "Sounds good. I'll check it out."

Sasha's grin widened, and for a moment, Cam forgot all about the record sleeve in his hand.

"So do you think you can help me with that? Do I have to order it or something?"

"Hmm? Oh, I don't know. Let me look on the system. We get heaps of this old crap in all the time. We might have it here."

"It's not crap, dude. It's a classic."

Cam rolled his eyes and took the old Beatles record to the computer on the vinyl side of the shop and tapped in his pass code. Sasha followed and stood beside him, close enough so Cam could smell the scents of bike oil and ocean breeze on him.

Nice.

The vinyl record came up on the computer screen. Bingo. They had it in stock. Cam logged off and pointed to a shelf loaded with vinyl records. "The system says it's somewhere up there. Might take me a while to find it. Do you need to get back to work?"

"I do, actually. Can I come by later and pick it up?"

"Works for me. If you're not back before three, I'll leave it behind the counter for you."

Sasha flashed another breathtaking grin, and this time Cam took note of the dimple in his left cheek. "That's awesome. Thanks, man. Check you later."

He punched Cam's shoulder and ambled to the door, leaving Cam to rub his tingling arm and spend the rest of his shift pondering just how much of Sasha's skin was touched by his deep, golden tan.

Later that evening, Cam's daydreaming got the better of him, and he came back to reality to find his father and older sister bickering over his head. About him, apparently, and his nonexistent plans for the future.

"Leave the boy alone, Kay. He came for his dinner, not an inquisition."

Cam shot his father a grateful look. His sister was the best, but she was like a dog with a damned bone when she had her mind set on something. Jesus. That would teach him for stopping by on a weekday evening. He was prepared for this shit on a Sunday.

Kay huffed. "Let me talk, Dad." She ruffled Cam's hair, and her expression softened. "I'm just saying, you graduated college three years ago. If you're not going to do anything with that degree, you should probably do something else. Find a nice man. Settle down, and give Dad some grandbabies. I was reading about surrogacy in—"

"Kay, stop." Cam groaned and laid his head on the kitchen counter. This was the con of having an open-minded family who knew and accepted every facet of his life—they had an opinion on everything too. "I'm not seeing anyone right now, and even if I was, I wouldn't be hustling them down the sperm bank."

He was saved by the oven timer. Kay turned away to deal with the bubbling lasagna, and by the time Cam sat down to a rowdy family dinner with his dad, Kay, and his younger twin brothers, the subject had been left by the wayside.

After dinner, he cleaned up with his dad. "Thanks for the save with Kay. She's been on my case about that for weeks."

"The school thing?" Wade dried a chipped plate. Mom had taken all the good ones. "Don't worry about that. She just worries about you. She wants to see you settled."

"I am settled."

"Settled doing nothin'." Wade raised his hand. "And don't tell me making those adult art films makes you happy, because Lord knows, I don't think it does."

"Dad, just call it porn."

"Humor me."

Cam grinned. There were elements of Blue Boy that were considered artistic—the location scenes, and the scripts Jon sometimes wrote, but he figured his pop's idea of porn involved rubber police uniforms and bad mustaches. "What pearl of wisdom are you trying to get out?"

"None, today at least. I think you've had enough of that from your sister. I'm just saying you've been working at the store awhile now, and doing your…filming. Maybe it's time to branch out."

Wade said no more, but that was typical of him. He liked to drop a bomb of astute philosophy on the table and let it fester. He'd come back to it in six months' time and expect Cam to have an answer.

Still, it could've been worse, a lot worse. Cam's family had fragmented in two, but what remained was strong and real. Not like the broken mess of Levi's childhood or the hotbed of rejection that had driven Sonny all the way to LA. Cam couldn't imagine a world without his family. His parents had been married thirty years, and they hadn't made it through, but the love that remained was the most important love of all.

They finished the dishes in companionable silence, and after, Wade shuffled off to watch his fishing show, leaving Cam to contemplate what to do with the rest of his evening. With the next day's shoot looming, he felt keyed up and restless, like he wanted to stay up all night, hanging out, playing pool, or shooting the breeze with someone who just…got him.

On cue, his phone vibrated in his pocket. A message from Jon. *Midnight. My place.*

Cam stared at the text with a strange sensation in the pit of his belly. He craved companionship and warmth, but somehow, even though his night was sure to end connected to the body of another, he'd never felt more alone.

CHAPTER THREE

"Are you ready?"

Cam met Jon's gaze with a scowl. "Ready for what? All I'm doing is lying on a fucking couch."

"Are you going to be like this all day?"

"Like what?"

Jon fixed him with a steady glare. "Forget it. Just be on set in five. Matthew's ready."

Cam stared after Jon's retreating back, frustrated. He knew he was being a brat, but he couldn't help it. Jon brought out the worst in him when they were at odds, and even sometimes when they weren't. Bitter and bitchy—that's how he felt, and he didn't like it. He didn't like it at all.

A sleepless night didn't help. He'd answered Jon's midnight summons, only to be sidelined by a phone call that just couldn't wait. Jon never came back to bed, and Cam gave up waiting at two a.m. and walked home to glare at his own bedroom ceiling and wonder when he'd become such a fucking loser.

Cam got to his feet with a heavy sigh, feeling the burn in his legs from a frustration-driven predawn gym session. It hadn't always been like this. He remembered the first time Jon coaxed him into bed…that balmy summer evening his dad had sat him down and told him his mom was leaving for good. Distraught, Cam had found himself drunk and alone at Silver, nursing his eleventieth shot of bourbon. Jon had taken him home and fucked him. Lit some candles and made him feel special…safe. Like the world as he knew it wasn't imploding. The storm passed, but sometimes he felt like he'd been chasing that relief ever since.

He stomped his way to the set. A few of the crew shot him curious glances, letting him know his rare bad mood was more than a little obvious. Jon ignored him entirely, and to distract himself, Cam cast his gaze around, looking for his partner in crime for the day. He didn't have to look far. On the couch at the back of the set sat Matthew, another dancer from Silver who'd made the transition to Blue Boy model.

Cam crossed the set and flopped down beside Matthew. His own frame was slim and athletic, but Matthew was petite and Cam dwarfed him. "'S'up."

Matthew returned his fist bump. "Hey, man. How's it going?"

"Same old, same old." Cam wasn't about to pour his heart out. "You all set for today? Got any questions? Limits? Shit you don't like?"

"Nope, I'm good." Matthew grinned, showing Cam a set of perfect white teeth. With inky hair and green eyes too similar to Cam's own to hold any intrigue, he wasn't Cam's type at all. "I told Jon I was ready to dive right in, but he said I had to shoot a foreplay scene first."

"Really?" Dampening down eagerness wasn't Jon's usual MO. Cam filed the information away for later. "Well, it might be foreplay, but we can make it good. Sure there's nothing you don't want to do?"

Matthew shook his head. "I'm game for anything."

Cam rolled his eyes, wondering if the kid knew no one was listening, though it was possible he meant every word. Some models *didn't* care what happened to their bodies on set. In fact, some of them craved the pounding some of the tops liked to give out. Still, though Jon would've covered all bases, Cam always made a point of asking, even when he filmed with a model he knew well. Shit like that could change in a heartbeat, and he didn't want to be the bastard who gave a guy nightmares.

"How's the dancing going? You gonna keep it up now you've moved over here?"

Matthew stretched out his legs. "Probably. Sonny and Kai do both, right? And Sonny's in college too, so it can't be that hard."

Give it time. "See how you feel. You might find the extra cash isn't worth the effort."

"Maybe." Matthew shrugged. "Someone told me you're a dancer too, but I haven't seen you around."

"I don't dance anymore. I used to, back in the day, but I gave it up. It wasn't really my scene."

Like porn, Cam had fallen into dancing on podiums in the clubs by accident. It was fun and a cheap way to party. He didn't have half the moves the headhunted dancers at Silver did, but he could work a pole well enough.

"You're too big to be a dancer anyway. Most of us are tiny, except Sonny, and he's still pretty compact."

Cam snickered. "Trust me. Sonny ain't *that* small."

Matthew grinned and the conversation moved on, but an odd sensation crept into Cam's belly. He felt strange, like he could climb out of his own skin.

"Everybody ready?"

Cam nodded without meeting Jon's gaze, his mind already on autopilot. He counted down in his head. *Five. Four. Three. Two. One…*

"Action!"

Matthew slid into Cam's lap like a snake, and his lips were on Cam's without preamble, negating any need for staged banter.

Cam went with the flow, like he did most scenes, relaxing into the kiss and letting his hands roam Matthew's supple body, getting a feel for him and searching for the common ground that would bring them together.

Matthew worked his lips down Cam's neck and tugged at his T-shirt. Cam pulled it over his head and returned the gesture, taking in the bold and bright tattoos stamped on Matthew's torso. They were like badges, or robots, maybe…Cam couldn't tell.

Cam frowned on the inside. Most of the smaller models were inked up these days, but Sonny aside, tattoos didn't do it for him. He much preferred naked skin, those swathes of flesh where he could see the true shape of a man—the curves of muscle and bone…

Matthew bit down on Cam's nipple. Cam shuddered, and his dick hardened, slow and sure. He liked teeth—grazing and nipping. He moaned to let Matthew know he was on the right track. Matthew bit him again, moving lower and lower until he came to Cam's waistband.

Cam raised his hips in response. "Fuck, yeah."

The scene continued, following a loose but predictable routine. Clothes disappeared, the leather couch squeaked, and before long Cam found himself on his back, his dick in Matthew's mouth, and Matthew's dick and ass hovering over his face.

He blew Matthew for a while, enjoying his thighs quivering and tensing around his shoulders. What Matthew lacked in on-screen experience, he made up for in enthusiasm. He was good with his mouth and hands, and Cam let himself be carried away by the hot, wet heat of another man's tongue on his cock.

A distant pleasure began to coil in the pit of Cam's stomach. He pulled his mouth off Matthew's dick with wet *pop* and thrust his own hips up. "Yeah, like that, like that."

Matthew worked him harder. Cam closed his eyes and let it wash over him while he took a second to consider his options. Matthew had a nice ass, and he'd said he was up for anything…

Cam slid his index finger into his mouth and opened his eyes to find Jon watching him from behind the main camera. Was it his imagination, or did the man seem pissed?

What the fuck is his problem?

Cam deliberated a moment, then cut Jon out of his mind and pressed his spit-slick finger into Matthew, gauging his reaction to every twist and flick. Of all the facets of porn, this was probably what Cam, enjoyed the most—observing, fascinated, as each partner responded differently to his touch.

Sometimes he got carried away and found himself pondering the possible correlations between events in a man's real life and his behavior on the set, but not today. Today he was still squirming from his unsatisfactory encounter the night before, and he needed to fucking come.

For a moment he considered rearranging the whole scene and pushing his cock inside Matthew's tight body. It had been so long since he'd topped, the image in his head sent a shiver of energy through his overheated body. He looked around for condoms and lube. On set, such things were never far away.

Jon caught his eye, read his intentions, and shook his head. The message was clear. *Not today.*

Anger surged through Cam, but Matthew chose that moment to grind down on Cam's fingers, blocking Jon from view. "I'm gonna come."

Cam focused and wrapped his free hand around Matthew's dick. He wasn't even close, but that was easily fixed once Matthew shot his load. Cam twisted his fingers, finding the bundle of nerves inside Matthew and tickled it in time with each pass of his thumb over the head of Matthew's cock.

It didn't take long. Matthew yelped and spilled on Cam's chest, shivering like he'd never felt such a thing before. Maybe he hadn't. Cam watched him shudder with a wry smile. The number of bottoms he'd come across who'd never had their prostate touched often bemused him. How the hell did they live?

"Your turn."

Cam shifted on the couch, making his dick more accessible. Matthew took him in his mouth and set a fast pace that should've made Cam come with little trouble. But it didn't happen, and for a while release kept itself out of reach, teasing Cam with its nearness.

Impatient and feeling Jon's eyes on him, Cam gave Matthew a hand, literally, and relief swept over him when he came with a quiet cry. The last jolts of orgasm eased, and after, he lay still and stared at the ceiling, ignoring the bustle of the cleanup crew. He'd been craving this for days, but instead of satiation, he felt edgy and unfulfilled, and his balls felt heavy, like he'd only blown half his load. The logical part of his brain knew such a thing was impossible. Coming was coming, right? So why did he feel so damned unsatisfied?

Friday
Act(s)—Kissing, blowjobs, handjobs. Ass play (not mine)
Partner(s)—Matthew
???? I don't know. I used to feel upbeat after every scene. Energized, like I could take on the world. Today I feel like some fucker turned me inside out without ever laying a finger on me. It's not Matthew's fault, or even Jon's. I'm just in a weird place right now, and I don't know why. I feel strange. Like my skin's not my own.

It's been like this for a while now. After every shoot I feel more and more like I've only done half a job...like I've missed out on something or forgotten to do something really fucking important. Lol. Or maybe I need to rearrange those words. Maybe fucking has become too important to me.

Does this mean I should quit porn? Who knows? Maybe Levi. I'd ask him if the dude ever picked up his phone.

Cam sat back and squinted at the scrawl in his journal. The entry was shorter than his usual ramblings, but he had nothing else to say. He'd left the studio without watching the rest of the scenes unfold, and hit the gym again, hoping to dispel the discontent lingering in his veins, but it hadn't worked. Instead he'd found himself more restless than ever and unable to decipher his mood.

He set down his pen with a sigh. Perhaps that was the point. He'd been keeping a diary since he'd confessed his fledgling porn career to a fellow psych student a few years back. The chick had asked him to record his thoughts and feelings for a month or so, so she could analyze them for her thesis. He'd agreed, and three years later, it was a habit he'd yet to crack. The thick, spiral-bound notebook cataloged every scene or encounter he'd ever been paid to perform.

On occasion, he flipped through the scribbled accounts, trying to track his state of mind from month to month, year to year, but it had been a while, and today he was a little scared of what he might find. Had he really become such a fiend that he was only happy if he was banging the world?

Man, he hoped not. Porn star he may've been, but there was more to life than sex. There had to be, 'cause Lord knew he wasn't getting any. At least not the kind that mattered.

Quasi Sonny popped into his mind. *"Real sex—the kind where someone looks at you like you're their whole world. You don't get that in porn, Cam."*

CHAPTER FOUR

"Long time, no see."

Cam glanced up as a BMX skidded to a stop beside him. Sasha, the hot Beatles fan, greeted him with a wide grin. "Hey."

Cam smiled back. It was early, as always, and he was kneeling outside the Beat Shak, cleaning the A-Board sign. Sasha's smiling face was a welcome surprise. Cam had missed his return trip to the store last week. "Hey yourself."

"Whatcha doing?"

"Cleaning, dude. What does it look like?"

Sasha made a face that set a spark somewhere deep inside Cam. A spark that made him giddy.

Huh.

"It's too early for cleaning, man." Sasha looked up at the sky. "Come for a ride."

Cam stood and took in the sight of Sasha astride his bike. With his broad shoulders and sun-lightened hair, it was quite a picture. "No can do. I'm the only one here, *and* I don't think my board would keep up with you."

"True. How about later? I'll lend you a bike, if you're game enough to ride with me."

Sasha was definitely gay. Cam knew even before the subtle flirtation lacing the challenge hit him full force. "What time?"

"Anytime after four. I'm the boss. I can do what I like."

Sasha stood up on his pedals and rolled off the sidewalk, zipping away before Cam found his tongue.

Cam wondered into the store in a daze. Did that really just happen? Despite the distraction of the studio, he'd thought of Sasha a lot since they'd met the week before. The guy was hot, and he had a grin that lit up Cam's world, where genuine grins, untainted by lights and cameras, were in short supply.

He'd kind of figured he'd never see Sasha again, though. After all, Sasha's BMX store had been in business a few years, and Cam had *never* set eyes on him before. He would've remembered.

Still, Sasha's rugged allure aside, the idea of a ride was tempting. Cam hadn't hit a BMX ramp for ages, and the thrill was something he couldn't deny.

At least, that's what he told himself when he clocked off shift at four thirty p.m. and skated the two short blocks to Tate's Bikes.

Sasha met him with that damned grin and thrust a bike at him with little preamble. "Race you to the Basin."

It took a while for Cam to find his rhythm. Boarding came to him like breathing, but the bike was a different animal. His muscles burned, and the speed blew his mind. It was terrifying, and he loved it.

And it wasn't long before he caught up with Sasha.

Cam followed him along the seafront until he veered off back inland to the local skate park. Cam pulled up as Sasha hit the ramps, watching as Sasha nailed a few tricks. The guy was good, though Cam reckoned he could match him any day on his skateboard.

When Cam had caught his bearings, he rolled his borrowed BMX through the tube a few times, paying heed to Sasha's shouted instructions in the vain hope he wouldn't fall on his ass.

It worked, for a while, until he took a jump too fast and skidded into Sasha, sending them both clattering into the railing at the top of the concrete ramp.

Sasha took it with good humor, though the surprise on his face made Cam laugh so hard his eyes watered. The guy was graceful, given his size, and he looked funny as hell beneath an upside-down bike.

"Dick." Sasha gave Cam a playful shove. "Good thing we just met, or I'd put you on your ass."

Sasha's choice of words calmed Cam's laughter. He was so at ease with Sasha it felt like he'd known him for years, and for some reason it unnerved him a little.

Cam gave himself an internal shake. What was up with that? So what if they clicked? It wasn't a crime. The opposite, in fact. "Try it."

"Maybe later." Sasha set his bike down and sat on the edge of the ramp. "How long have you worked at Beat Shak?"

"A few years." Cam sat and mirrored Sasha's posture, dangling his legs down the ramp. "I got the job straight out of college. Never figured out what to do next."

"Me either. That's why I set up the store, to earn some cash while I fucked around with bikes."

Cam tilted his face to the sky, absorbing the late afternoon sun. "Worked out all right though, didn't it? Your place is rammed on the weekends."

"We do okay. Keeps me outta trouble, anyway."

"You don't look like trouble."

"Tell that to my mom. She blames me for every gray hair she's ever had."

Cam laughed, though he sounded hollow to his ears. He loved his mom, but the bitterness he felt for her desertion just wouldn't quit. He hadn't spoken to her since she'd packed up half their family home and jumped ship to "find" herself. "Bet she wouldn't have you any other way."

"Most days. You want to get something to eat?"

Cam checked his watch. He had a dinner date with Sonny, if Sonny remembered to show up this time. Maybe they could go to Levi's and hustle some real food out of the big man.

"Do you need to get to work?"

"Hmm?" Cam leaned away, startled. He hadn't noticed himself drifting closer to Sasha. "No, I'm done for the day."

"I didn't mean that." Sasha fiddled with his bike wheel. "I meant your, er, other job."

Cam frowned, glad Sasha seemed distracted and couldn't see the uncharacteristic flush heating his face. He made no secret of his unconventional occupation, but the words felt weird coming from Sasha. Somehow, he'd detached the best afternoon he'd had in months from his reality. "I didn't know you recognized me."

Sasha turned back with a shrug, though his grin seemed different, muted somehow. "Every gay man in LA knows who you are."

That wasn't news to Cam. He'd become accustomed to the attention he got in Silver, or any other club he ever ventured to. He'd even grown used to the stares in the grocery store and the whispers when fans discovered him working at Beat Shak and spent all afternoon peering through the windows at him. The scrutiny had never bothered him, but for some reason Sasha's fading grin felt like the end of the world. "I'm not *that* well-known."

"I reckon you are. I knew you were here long before we crossed paths."

"Yeah? How long?"

Sasha shrugged. "I heard a rumor a few years ago. Rode past here a few times, but I wasn't sure until I saw you up close in the store."

Cam tried to ignore the strange resentment brewing in his belly. He'd never cared if anyone knew he was in porn before. He'd told his own father without breaking a sweat, and his reaction to Sasha knowing confused him. Big-time. He wasn't ashamed of what he did, far from it. So why was this different? Why did he feel that the harder Sasha stared at him, the more unworthy Cam became of his attention? Cam had no idea, and the more he tried to decipher the whirlwind taking hold in his mind, the less he understood it. All he knew was something felt wrong…really wrong, with Sasha looking at him and seeing a goddamned porn star.

"Earth to Cam?" Sasha waved his hand in front of Cam's face. "You okay?"

Cam refocused. Tried to ignore the gentle warmth in Sasha's gaze. Ten minutes ago, he'd basked in it. Now he couldn't stand it. He retrieved his bike, stood up on the pedals, and pointed back the way they'd come. "You ready to go? I've gotta bounce."

He let his bike roll down the ramp without waiting for Sasha's response.

Thnx for the ride. C.

Cam set his phone on the kitchen counter. He'd exchanged numbers with Sasha after the porn bombshell, but for some reason it had taken him two days to compose a simple message, and almost as long to hit Send.

And now he couldn't keep still. There was something about Sasha, something more than his sunny smile and friendly eyes. More than his infectious laugh and easy ways. Something that Cam couldn't deny or stop thinking about.

He picked up his phone. Stared at the blank screen. Put it down again. He'd gotten over the fact that Sasha knew about his alter ego, or at least put it to the back of his mind, but thinking about Sasha still made him antsy, and he couldn't figure out if he saw Sasha as a pot of gold or an unexploded bomb.

What the fuck? You just met the dude.

Cam calmed his seldom-indulged inner drama queen and opened the refrigerator, looking for supper. Sonny had rearranged their dinner from a few days before, but he'd canceled the rescheduled date at the last minute, blaming a forgotten exam. Cam could believe it, knowing Sonny as well as he did, but he figured it more likely Sonny had crawled into Levi's bed and decided to stay there.

And that wasn't necessarily a bad thing, 'cause Lord knew, Sonny needed the rest.

The contents of the fridge were uninspiring. Beer, cheese slices, and a dubious jar of pickles. Cam let the door swing shut and reached for his phone. Orange chicken and egg rolls would hit the spot. He ordered enough food to last until he next went home to his dad's. This cooking shit was for schmucks.

His phone vibrated as he tossed it on the countertop. He picked it up again, feeling his heart skip a beat as Sasha's Facebook photo lit up the screen. What was it about that guy with the sun behind him?

Fucking magic, that's what it was.

Cam opened the message.

UR welcome. Might feed you next time.

Next time? Cam drummed his fingers on the countertop and tapped out a message. *What would you feed me?*

A message pinged right back. *Anything not from a packet.*

Cam tapped the image of Sasha's smiling face and waited for the call to connect. He didn't have to wait long.

"'Lo?"

"Still judging me by that burrito, huh?"

Sasha laughed. "Hell, yeah. That shit was nasty."

"Nah. That was lunch. I had a cheeseburger for dinner."

Sasha made a noise that sounded a little too like Levi for Cam's liking. "What did you have for dinner tonight?"

"Nothing yet." Cam glanced at the clock. "It's only eight o'clock."

"And you're about to order pizza, right?"

"Chinese, actually."

"I gotta better idea. You got any other plans tonight, besides poisoning yourself with MSG?"

"That was about it." Cam opened the fridge again and grabbed a bottle of beer. "What have you got in mind?"

"Meet me by Beat Shak in an hour, and I'll show you."

Cam didn't need telling twice. He took the quickest shower known to man, canceled his food delivery, and jogged all the way to meet Sasha and his smug grin. Though he didn't discover the source of Sasha's amusement until they'd walked a few streets and Sasha pointed at a funky, glass-fronted restaurant.

"Sushi?"

Sasha's grin widened. "Yep. Don't tell me you're one of those freaks who live by the ocean and don't eat seafood."

Cam eyed the sushi bar with suspicion. "Hey, I eat fish. I just like it cooked."

"Don't knock it till you've tried it." Sasha held open the door to the restaurant. "And if you really can't handle it, some of the fish *is* cooked."

"I can handle it." Fuck. If he could handle a face full of spunk, he could handle a lump of raw fish.

Like his first ever blowjob, sushi turned out to be not that bad. Not that bad and kind of fun. Or maybe it was the company. Sasha laughed a lot and smiled even more. His good humor was irrepressible, and Cam found the antsy feeling he'd carried since the scene with Matthew at the studio faded away. Conversation was light and easy, and time passed in the blink of an eye.

At least until the elephant in the room made itself known.

"Sorry about dropping that porn shit on you last time."

Cam swallowed and set his water glass down. He'd been dreading this, the moment when his occupation tainted whatever was simmering between them. He measured his words with care. "I didn't know you knew."

"I didn't, at first. I wasn't sure. I had to check."

"How did you do that?"

"How do you think?"

Cam smirked; he couldn't help it. "Google?"

Sasha had the good grace to smirk right back. "I didn't have to look quite that far."

"You had me on your hard drive, huh?" Cam pushed his plate away, leaving only some weird floppy seaweed he couldn't quite stomach.

"Nothing recent. The scenes I have are a few years old."

"What happened? Did you grow out of your porn habit?"

Sasha put his elbows on the table. Despite the uncharacteristic nerves flickering in Cam's belly, Sasha seemed at ease, like this was a conversation he had every day. "My ex had a thing for Levi Ramone. Think he crushed on him more than he ever did me."

"Everyone's gotta thing for Levi."

"He is pretty hot, if you like 'em big and brawny."

"You don't?"

Sasha shrugged. "I don't know about porn stars, but I like a man with a brain."

Cam bristled like he had so many times before. "Levi's got more brains than all of us. Just never had a chance to use them."

"Shame. It's never too late though, right?" Sasha shifted. His leg brushed Cam's. "It's nice that you're friends. I've seen you around with that tattooed kid too. What's his name?"

"Sonny?"

"Yeah, that's him. I thought he was your boyfriend."

"We're just friends."

Sasha snorted, amused. "With benefits? Hassle-free hookups gotta be a perk of the job."

Cam couldn't deny it, and he didn't want to. Sasha seemed a laid-back kind of guy, and what was the point in lying to him? Friendships…relationships based on bullshit always went wrong. "I've hooked up with Sonny, but we've never dated. He's with someone."

"What about you? Are you seeing anyone?"

Yeah. My boss, but you really don't want to know. "Not really."

"Sounds complicated."

Cam shrugged. He didn't want to talk about Jon, but Sasha's sympathetic gaze persuaded him. "Kind of. It's more…unhealthy, you know? We're not good for each other. There are no feelings there."

"Just sex, huh? We've all been there, dude, but if it's not good for your soul, sometimes, you gotta walk away." Sasha checked his watch. "Look at that. We've been talking about porn for like, fifteen minutes already."

"Sorry."

"Don't be. I brought it up. I didn't want you to think it bothers me, 'cause it doesn't. I might be a bit out of touch, but there's more to you than porn, right?"

Cam leaned forward, taking in Sasha's relaxed posture and knowing the guy was telling the truth. "You don't watch it anymore at all?"

"Not often. I kinda went off sex for a while. It's a long story."

For the first time since they met, Sasha's eyes flickered with something other than humor and warmth. Curiosity burned on the tip of Cam's tongue, but a waitress interrupted, and when she'd gone, the moment had passed.

Sasha slipped a credit card into the bill folder. "Wanna ditch this place and get ice cream?"

"Ice cream? After all the bullshit you gave me about frozen burritos?"

"Course." Sasha winked, and the faint sadness in his eyes was all but gone. "I'm only human, Cam. Same as any other man."

CHAPTER FIVE

Survive the sushi?
Just about. Thnx for dinner. C.
I had fun :)
Me 2. Do I get to pick next time? C.
Depends…
On? C.
On what u got in mind.
Wht u like doin? C.
Same as u, probly.
Like 2 prty? C.
Course I do.
Then come out to play, C.

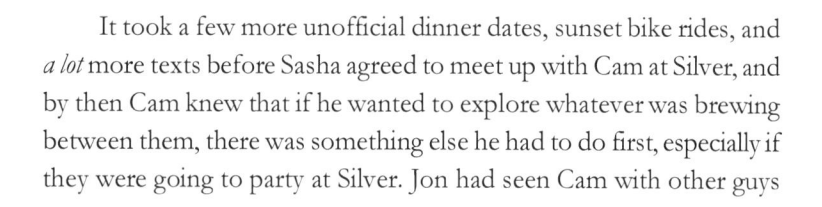

It took a few more unofficial dinner dates, sunset bike rides, and *a lot* more texts before Sasha agreed to meet up with Cam at Silver, and by then Cam knew that if he wanted to explore whatever was brewing between them, there was something else he had to do first, especially if they were going to party at Silver. Jon had seen Cam with other guys before and paid little heed, and Cam had seen him disappear down the stairs to his office enough times, but this was different. This was *Sasha*. They'd become firm friends, but Cam wanted more.

God, did he more. When they were apart, he thought of little else. Except for the unfinished business that led him to Jon's office door a few weeks after popping his sushi cherry.

The office was empty. Cam found Jon in the storeroom, rooting through old props. "Hey."

Jon glanced over his shoulder, his gaze curious. Cam didn't often seek him out of his own volition. It wasn't how they rolled. "Hey. Need something?"

"Are you busy?"

"I'm always busy, Cam. What's on your mind?"

Cam checked the corridor and shut the door, steeling himself, though for what, he wasn't quite sure. "I might come to the club on Friday."

"And?"

"And…" Cam measured his words. He'd come to the studio full of purpose, but without a foolproof plan in mind, and as ever, Jon had gotten under his skin with just a flick of his eyebrow. "I won't be alone."

Jon shoved a box back onto a shelving unit. Cam couldn't see his face, but he could picture the disinterest well enough. Even if Jon cared, it wasn't his way to let it show. "I'm going to chuck all this crap out." Jon held up a leather harness. "We don't shoot shit like this anymore. Times are changing. Folk want more than fucking these days. Roma-porn, that's what we're making here."

"Roma-porn? What the fuck is that? That ain't a thing."

Jon snorted. "Not yet. Maybe I could become a pioneer. I got a request for a scene following George and Zac on a date. A motherfucking date. Can you believe that shit? What happened to good old down and dirty?"

"That comes after, right?"

"Right." Jon dusted his hands on his jeans. "So what are you

35

trying to say? Are you seeing someone?"

Cam shrugged, perversely caught off guard by a conversation he'd instigated in the first place. "Maybe."

Jon closed the distance between them and put his hands on either side of Cam's head on the storeroom door, caging him. Cam swallowed, feeling his body betray him and respond to Jon's closeness. He wondered if Jon was the deciding factor, or if his senses were so conditioned by porn that any hot guy could make him hard.

Neither theory felt right. He wanted Sasha, damn it, not Jon.

Jon leaned closer. Cam could feel the heat from his skin. "What do you want me to say?"

"Nothing."

Jon stared at him, and for the first time since they'd come together last summer, Cam felt uncomfortable in his presence, like the buzzing current between them was something to be feared, not desired. An addiction that had run its course.

I don't want this.

The spell broke. Jon stepped back, and the intensity in his eyes faded, almost like he'd turned it off. Perhaps he had. "Cam, it's fine. You think you're the only one I tie to my bed?"

No. Cam had never thought that. Deep down he'd always known he was nothing more to Jon than a passing amusement, but something in Jon's demeanor bothered him. He hadn't expected Jon to profess his undying love, but the conversation had been easy…too easy. Jon didn't like to lose. Beneath the cool exterior, he was the ultimate alpha male.

"So we're cool? I mean, it's cool if I bring someone to the club, right?"

"Yeah, Cam. We're cool."

Cam dropped his empty bottle on the shiny bar top. It wobbled from side to side, precariously, but remained upright. Cam watched it with muted interest, ignoring the chatter of whoever occupied the stool beside him. Sasha had yet to show his face, and Cam was buzzed and *bored*.

He cast his gaze around the teeming club. The writhing bodies on the packed dance floor. The cluster of hard-core Blue Boy fans gathered around the podiums. And beyond, in the darker corners of Silver, the smattering of couples, no doubt bound for the private rooms at the back of the club.

Cam smirked and ordered another drink. He'd had some fun in those rooms over the years, but it had been a while. Outside of the studio, he'd been with no one but Jon for months.

But that's over now.

His fourth beer slid down like a dream. The pounding music ratcheted up a notch, and despite keeping his gaze trained on the door, Cam began to unwind, losing himself in the heady thrum that made Silver the hottest gay club in town. The dark dubstep bass line vibrated through his feet and shook his soul, teasing the long dormant part of him that used to dance the night away in this very club and others. The part of him that reveled in the sensation of a body gyrating against him, restrained only by a thin layer of cloth and the crowds of people around them.

Damn it. Drinking on an empty stomach always made Cam reflective…reflective and horny, and shit like that got him in trouble. Got him an apartment full of sweaty bodies he couldn't resist and a hangover that kicked his ass, though it had been a while since he'd hosted an impromptu Blue Boy party at his place.

Jon again…

But despite the sultry air of Silver working its magic, as Cam gazed out over the club, he didn't miss the hedonistic nights he'd enjoyed in the past. Something had changed in him over the past year, and though he craved the touch of another man, he wanted more.

A warm arm draped over his shoulders. "Drinking alone?"

Sasha slid into the space beside him like he'd been there all along. Cam grinned like an idiot, giddy and so happy to see him he felt like his face would split in half. "Thought you'd bailed on me."

"Nah, just had to wait for Chris to get his drunk on enough to come with me."

Sasha jerked his head somewhere behind them, blond hair gleaming under the club's lights. Cam looked around and saw Sasha wasn't alone. With him was a burly guy whose wide eyes told Cam he was straight as a goddamned arrow. "How drunk was that? He doesn't look so happy."

"He's fine. It's not the first time he's come over to the dark side. He likes it, really."

"What about you?"

"Me?" Sasha let his arm drop from Cam and signaled the nearest bartender. "I like *you*. That's enough for me."

Cam felt warm from the inside out. Sasha had that effect on him, even without saying shit like that. He chugged his beer, hoping Sasha wouldn't see the heat in his face in the murky light of the club. Sasha passed him another, and it was a pattern that continued for the rest of the evening. Sasha's friend Chris joined them for a while, but his tolerance for half-naked men squeezing his butt ran thin, and he cried off sometime around midnight.

Sasha didn't seem to notice him go. He leaned close to Cam and tucked his wayward auburn curls behind his ears. "Do you come here a lot?"

Cam shivered. Sasha was a well-built guy, tall and strong, but his touch was light, teasing. "I kinda have to. Hanging here is part of my contract. I don't mind, though. The DJ's good, and I get cheap drinks."

Sasha glanced around. They hadn't moved from their spot since he'd arrived, but the scenery around them had changed as the night wore on. It was Cam's habit to hang by the far end of the bar, close to the podiums and DJ booth. Most of the Blue Boy models gravitated that way too, and though Sasha claimed he didn't watch much porn, he was bound to recognize some of the faces close by.

The other models had certainly noticed him, and who wouldn't? Sasha was gorgeous, and only amusement kept Cam from decking the parade of guys who'd approached them throughout the night.

Amusement and the fact that Sasha dismissed each one without tearing his gaze from Cam.

Cam reached for his drink. His arm brushed Sasha's. Sasha caught his eye and grinned, letting Cam know he felt the spark between them too. Cam's beer bottle was empty, and the current in the air had him suddenly restless.

Cam grabbed Sasha's hand, leaned close, and held his lips over Sasha's ear. "Wanna split?"

In answer, Sasha squeezed his hand and inclined his head toward the exit. "Lead the way."

It took a while to weave through the throng of sweaty, writhing bodies. Cam was stopped from time to time, asked to sign skin and pose for photos, and forced to dodge the advances of smitten fans. Most settled for a kiss on the cheek, but others were harder to shake off. Sasha took it all in his stride, or at least he seemed to until he found a gap in the crowd and pushed Cam against the wall.

"Okay, enough of this bullshit. When do *I* get to kiss you?"

Cam swallowed, enjoying the sensation of Sasha's bigger frame surrounding him. "You can kiss me."

"Oh yeah?" Sasha took Cam's face in his hands. Despite the heat of the club, his palms were dry as a bone. "What about if I kiss you like this?"

Sasha kissed Cam, slow and deep, a brush of lips at first, and then a gentle sweep of his tongue that turned Cam's limbs liquid.

Cam fell slack against the wall. They kissed over and over, hands grasping, clothes hitched. Sasha broke away for air, but Cam pulled him back and shoved his fingers into Sasha's silky hair.

The club faded away. Sasha, the smell of him, the feel of him, became Cam's whole world. He slid his hands under Sasha's shirt, found the smooth skin of his strong chest and rippled abdomen, and felt the solid outline of his cock, hard against his leg. Cam's own dick throbbed in his jeans. Silver was a den of shameless Epicureanism, and they could've fucked right there on the edge of the dance floor and not drawn much attention to themselves, but Cam didn't want that, not with Sasha. He wanted to take Sasha home, lay him out on his bed, and explore every inch of him until he eased himself down on Sasha's thick cock…

Huh. I want to bottom for this guy.

The thought didn't feel strange or frightening. It felt right, so fucking right. Cam tugged on Sasha's hips, grinding them together, before he slipped a hand between them and squeezed Sasha's dick. Sasha moaned into Cam's mouth and nipped his bottom lip. Encouraged, Cam moved his hand lower and lower until he grazed Sasha's balls.

Sasha froze. The air shifted. An abrupt change of atmosphere that hit Cam in the chest. Sasha pulled away like he'd been burned, his eyes wide and stricken.

Cam frowned, feeling the heat between them evaporate. What the fuck? Had he pushed too hard, hurt Sasha in some way? He reached out, his hands open in a placating gesture. Sasha hesitated, and the mist in his gaze seemed to clear, but before they could regroup, someone else called Cam's name.

Irritated, Cam looked beyond Sasha for the first time since they'd embraced. His ire increased when he spotted Jon heading his way. Jon didn't often venture out of the back-room areas, and Cam had hoped to avoid him entirely.

Jon appeared at his side. "Where's Sonny?"

"What?"

"Don't give me that." Jon leaned into Cam's personal space, ignoring Sasha, who took the hint and backed away before Cam could stop him. "Where the fuck is your little boy toy? He was due onstage a half hour ago, and that's the third time he's skipped out on me this month."

Cam flinched; he couldn't help it. He wasn't scared of Jon, but the raw aggression in his tone was unnerving. Cam could tell he'd been hitting the scotch. "I don't know where Sonny is."

"Bullshit." Jon tossed a glance over his shoulder. "I know you're tight with that kid. Does your new trick know you'll be screwing Sonny on the side?"

"Fuck you." Cam twisted away, but Jon caught his arm. "Get off me."

Jon released him with a smirk, casting his gaze again over Sasha. "Have it your way. Shame, 'cause he's got a look I like. Bring him by my place if you change your mind. I know you like to share."

Cam shoved past Jon without looking back. His skin crawled. Jon could be a hard-ass, but Cam had never seen him so overbearing and possessive. Or had he? Was that what had been going on all this time? Had Jon controlled him in more ways than he'd ever known?

Cam reached Sasha and realized he didn't care. All that mattered was Sasha, and it was clear by the other man's face he'd heard every word of Jon's bizarre rant. "Sorry about that."

Sasha opened his mouth and shut it again, his expression torn. He gestured for Cam to follow him to the exit.

Clear air hit Cam, cooling his skin and dispersing the booze-fueled haze from his mind. He took a deep breath and waited for Sasha to face him.

He felt sick when he saw the resignation in Sasha's eyes.

"That's the guy you've been seeing, isn't it?" Sasha's tone was flat and defeated but held no malice or accusation.

Cam winced. It wasn't his nature to lie, and he couldn't deny it. "I'm not seeing him anymore. We broke it off a few days ago."

"Does he know that? 'Cause he was looking at me like I raped his momma."

"He knows. He's cool."

"It didn't look cool, Cam. It looked like unfinished business."

Cam was silent. What more could he say? He'd been honest with Jon and taken him at his word that there were no hard feelings between them. They'd hardly shared an epic love affair. Cam wanted to punch Jon, but he knew the blame lay with him for bringing Sasha into Jon's turf. For bringing Sasha into the melting pot of his alter ego's lifestyle.

"Listen." Sasha touched Cam's arm, then let his hand fall away. "Maybe we should cool it a little."

"What? No, don't say that. I'm sorry, okay? I shouldn't have brought you here. This place is intense."

"I don't care about all this shit. There's more to you than porn. I can see that. I just can't get involved with a guy who's still tied to someone else. I like you, Cam, I really like you, but I can't get hurt like that."

Cam felt his heart sink slowly into the pit of his stomach. "What are you saying?"

"I'm saying, I think we should just be friends."

"Friends?"

"Yeah, friends. Maybe you need one you don't fuck." The words stung, but before Cam could retaliate, Sasha shook his head and groaned. "Shit. I didn't mean that."

Cam snorted. "So what did you mean? That I'm a freakin' man whore?"

Guilt colored Sasha's features before he caught it and schooled his expression, but Cam saw it like a goddamned billboard sign. Sasha didn't want to fuck a dirty, used porn star.

"Cam, I didn't mean—"

"Save it." Cam held up his hand. "It's cool, okay? What do you think I'm gonna do? Force you?"

Sasha said nothing for a long moment; then he sighed, and the defeat in his long-drawn-out breath washed over Cam like a cold wave on a cloudy day. "I'm going home, Cam. I'll see you around."

CHAPTER SIX

Cam threw his phone across the living room. It landed on the couch, bouncing along the cushions until it came to an anticlimactic stop. He glared at it, perhaps in the hope its spontaneous flight would stimulate it into life, but nothing happened. The screen remained as blank as it had been for the two long weeks since Sasha had left him hanging outside Silver.

Though he'd done nothing to break it, the silence had driven Cam kind of crazy, and it wasn't just Sasha who hadn't called. Jon hadn't sent through his monthly schedule, and Sonny was proving elusive too. Cam was too pissed to care about Jon—he'd show his face soon enough—but Sonny's absence worried him. Sonny had issues, and Cam would've bet his right arm that Levi knew nothing about them. Sonny was a spiky ray of light to those lucky enough to be close to him, but life had taught him to play his cards close to his chest.

With a heavy sigh, Cam stomped into his battered sneakers and retrieved his phone. Despite his black mood, it hadn't been entirely silent. His dad had checked in, calling him home for Sunday dinner, and however deep the funk he was in, it was a call he couldn't ignore. Sunday was the day he tried to put his crazy life aside, when scheduling allowed, and went back to his old life…the life before porn. He wasn't in the mood to flick meatballs at his siblings, but perhaps he needed to do just that.

He took a cab to his old family home with the situation with Sasha still heavy on his mind. Wade took one look at him and folded him into the kind of embrace most fathers didn't bother to give out, especially to their adult sons, but Wade was different. Always had been.

"Come and help me with dinner, Son. I could use the company."

Cam gave his brothers quick high fives and followed Wade into the kitchen. The smell of pot roast hit him with a wave of nostalgia. In the old days, slow-roasted beef in gravy was the only thing Wade ever cooked. Man, how times had changed. Without a wife, the old dude had learned fast. Chicken sticks, pizza rolls, grilled cheese. The world was his oyster now.

"Peel some carrots. Your brothers need some vitamins."

Wade ambled to the stove, leaving Cam with a pile of vegetables and a heavy heart. Sasha was always saying shit like that. The guy had a junk-food phobia, and his attempts to wean Cam from his diet of takeout and beer was a running joke between them. Sushi, super salads, raw foods. Over the past month, Cam had tried them all.

"Are you going to tell your old dad what has your bottom lip stuck out so far?"

"Hmm?" Cam dumped a pile of sliced carrots in a pot, carrots he knew only Kay would touch. "I'm fine, Pops. Just tired."

Wade didn't answer immediately. He pottered around, getting plates from the cupboards and setting them out on a thick oak table that was older than Cam. The sight of it reminded Cam just how long his parents had been together before his mom grew tired of family life.

"Your sister's going to be late. She's got a yoga class or something."

"On Sunday?"

Wade rolled his eyes and stirred the mashed potatoes. "She's committed. Sometimes I think she's as bat-shit crazy as you are."

Cam took the ribbing with good grace. In many ways, Wade was his best friend. "Least the downward dog doesn't make her damaged goods."

"Trouble with your love life, Son?"

Cam followed Wade to the table and flopped into a chair. "Something like that."

"How so?" Wade slid a glass of lemonade across the table. "I thought you weren't looking for anyone while you had this other…job."

"When did I say that?"

"When I gave you a ride home from the airport a few months back, remember? When you went to New York?"

Cam snorted. The Blue Boy trip to New York had happened just after the infamous scene between Levi and Rex. Both models had severed their contracts, and to stave off gossip, Jon had taken a group of his most popular models to New York to hook up with another studio. A distraction of the best kind. Cam hadn't performed much in front of the ever-present cameras, but a private party in Jon's hotel room had gone on for days. It was still going when he left early to return to his job at Beat Shak, and he'd been up for thirty-six hours by the time his dad picked him up from LAX. "I probably said a lot of things then."

"Not really." Wade sliced some bread and pushed the board to the middle of the table. "And you've been out of sorts ever since. What happened? Did you meet someone?"

Cam glanced toward the den, but his brothers were engrossed in computer games and paying the kitchen no heed. "Kinda, but not then, and he's not from the studio. I met him at Beat Shak. He's got a BMX store a few blocks away."

"What's his name?"

"Sasha." Cam smiled. It felt good to say his name aloud, even if his absence was an open wound. "He's real nice, Pops. Laid-back, cool. You'd like him."

"I like all your friends, Son. Even the one that talks my ear off."

Sonny. Everyone loved Sonny. "Sasha likes the same music as you. All that sixties crap."

"Even better. So why the long face?"

"He wants to be *friends*."

Wade took a seat and leaned back on his chair. "What's wrong with that? Friends is good, right?"

"I guess." Cam put his head on his arms. "I just… For a while, it seemed like he wanted more, you know?"

"Did something happen?"

Cam shrugged. Wade was the best dad in the world, but Cam couldn't tell him about Jon. His father was an old hippie at heart, and he'd never understand the hold Jon had over Cam, or why Cam found it so hard to break.

Wade nodded, like the gap in the tale made perfect sense to him. "If you really believe there's something between you, I guess you gotta figure out what spooked him. If he's as chill as you say he is, something besides the, er, movies must have scared him off."

Cam ignored the bizarreness that was his father describing anything as *chill* and considered his theory. Something clicked in his mind. Wade was right. The fear had been in Sasha's eyes before Jon barged between them. But why? What did Sasha have to be afraid of? Him? Porn? Commitment? It didn't make any sense. Cam had asked nothing of him, and he'd seen no hesitation in Sasha until that fuck-hot kiss against the wall.

Wade sighed and clapped his shoulder. "Maybe it's time you looked beyond this place that's got you tied up so tight. Money ain't everything. Fix what you can. Don't wait for other folk to do it for you."

Cam split soon after dinner, his father's sage advice ringing in his ears. With that in mind, he stopped at Sonny's place on his way home, but there was no one there. His cell went straight to voice mail, and his call to Levi didn't even connect.

Worry tickled again at Cam's belly. Sonny was a big boy, figuratively, at least, and capable of looking after himself, but sometimes he just…didn't. Perhaps it was time Cam grew a pair and stopped by Levi's motorcycle garage and touched base. It had been a while.

Resolved, Cam headed for home with a mind to bite the bullet and call Sasha too. Friends. He could do that, right? It was, after all, exactly what they'd been doing, just without the kissing. Or any prospect of kissing. Huh. Perhaps Wade was right and Cam *did* need to expand his life outside the studio. Porn used to be fun, a way of exploring his sexual identity and having a good time, but these days it seemed like a vise around his soul.

He missed Sasha. Sonny was his friend, Levi too, but though it had never seemed to matter before, Cam knew those friendships were colored by sex. His friendship with Sasha was real, like nothing he'd ever known, and without it, he felt lost. He'd seen other models lose relationships because of porn, but he never thought it would happen to him.

So do something about it.

Cam let himself into his apartment with his phone tucked between his chin and his shoulder. The call rang and rang until Sasha's voice mail kicked in. Cam's heart skipped a beat, jarred by Sasha's deep voice rumbling down the line. He considered hanging up, calling again and again until Sasha picked up or threw his phone at a damned wall, but he didn't.

"Hey, it's Cam. I'm sorry about the other night. Maybe you're right about being friends. I've gotta spare board if you'd dig a skate sometime this week. You can show me those tricks you think I can't do. Call me."

He hung up the phone and let out the breath he'd been holding.

Putting the ball in Sasha's court felt good, like he'd taken a vital step forward, but his body felt tense and stiff. He needed a hot shower and an early night.

The jets of water worked their magic on his sore neck and shoulder muscles. Cam lingered under the spray. Sasha remained on his mind, but he tried to ignore the butterflies in his belly. Instead, he closed his eyes and soaped his body lazily, paying little attention as he passed his hands over his chest, abdomen, and lower. His cock hung limp between his legs, as uninspired as the rest of him, but he lingered a moment on his balls. He kept them shaved for porn—*manscaped* was the technical term—and the lack of body hair meant their outlined shape was fairly clear. Clear and *familiar*, so why did they feel different?

Perturbed, Cam pulled himself from his Sasha-filled daydreams, shut off the shower, and climbed out, wiping the steam from the mirror with the back of his hand. He turned this way and that, scrutinizing himself from every angle. His left ball had always hung lower and appeared larger, but in the misty bathroom mirror, the difference seemed disproportionate.

He cupped them in his hand, rolling them, squeezing them with gentle fingers. His balls were often sensitive, just a lick or a scratch from the right partner drove him wild, but there was nothing erotic about the sweat dripping down his back now. He focused on his left side, tracing the shape and texture. Was it his imagination, or did it feel too hard? Like a smooth rock had become lodged in his sac?

A rush of nausea swept over Cam. Dizzy, he stumbled back. He'd been on edge for days, and now the sensation of an intruder in his body was fusing with the sickening dread, merging the two emotions together and boiling over like angry, molten lava.

He sat down on the closed toilet, his heart beating like a drum in his ears. He was mistaken. He had to be, because the alternative was something he couldn't begin to imagine.

CHAPTER SEVEN

"I'm sorry, what?"

The doctor glanced up from his notes for the first time since he'd uttered a sentence Cam couldn't comprehend. "The lump in your testicle appears to be a tumor," the doctor repeated. "Combined with your blood work, I'd say it's a germ cell seminoma, but we need to run some more tests to be sure."

"Tests?" The word fell from Cam's lips with no conscious thought. He'd been at the doctor's office for less than an hour, and they were talking about fucking tumors? Screw this shit. He had to be freakin' tripping.

"Ultrasound, CT, chest X-ray. We'll take some more blood too."

"What for?"

"To ascertain for sure what we're dealing with, what stage it is, how far it's spread, and the sooner we do that, the better. Cancers like this are highly treatable, if we catch them early."

Cam blinked. "Cancer?"

The doctor sighed and tapped his pen on the table. Cam didn't like him. He preferred the other guy, the doctor he'd seen at the start of the week...the one who told him he had nothing to worry about.

"It's most likely a cyst. We'll take some blood, but it's probably nothing."

"Yes, Mr. Shaw. It's highly probable you have testicular cancer."

Mr. Shaw. The rare use of his legal name startled him, like it always did, and it took a moment for the implication of the doctor's words to hit him. "Probable? You don't know for sure?"

"Not yet, but I'll get the tests we need set up right away, and we should know within a few days."

A few days. Cam felt sick and dizzy, like his brain was about to explode. How the fuck could he sit on this for *days* without knowing for sure what he was dealing with?

The doctor passed him a plastic cup of water. "It's a lot to take in, I know, but you have time on your side. Given your profession, it's likely the lump hasn't been there that long. I'd imagine you, or a…colleague would've noticed it."

Cam nodded. The doctor's slip didn't go unnoticed, but he couldn't bring himself to care. Porn and the extensive health benefits that came with a contract at Blue Boy was the only reason he was flipping his shit in a plush private clinic rather than cooling his heels at the county hospital. And the doctor wasn't wrong. He'd been heavily intimate with a bunch of guys in the last month. Someone would've noticed.

Jon would've noticed, right?

Even as Cam shook the doctor's hand and left the office, he knew he couldn't be sure. Sex with Jon had deteriorated to the point where neither of them seemed to care who the other was. Cam knew he wasn't Jon's only lover, and *he* was a damned porn star.

A porn star with testicular cancer.

The following morning, Cam returned to the clinic and let the medical staff put him through a barrage of tests. Most of them involved being exposed in the most intimate way possible, but being naked in front of a bunch of strangers didn't bother him. Why would it?

Cam let his mind wander as they poked and prodded him, thinking back to last night and the evening he'd spent alone, brooding his fate. Though he hadn't touched a drop, he felt like he'd gone three rounds with a bottle of Jack.

Perhaps his pseudo-drunk state had been to blame for the text message he'd sent Jon, and the exchange that followed.

I want to fuck in my next scene.
Schedule is done for this month.
Change it.
What's going on?
What do you care?

There had been a long pause between the last two messages, and Jon hadn't bothered to reply. Cam wondered what he'd have done, even if Jon had. Would he have called Jon up and told him everything? Told him *this*? Guess he'd never know.

"Cameron Shaw?"

Cam glanced up. He was sitting in an empty room, waiting to see the specialist who'd tell him the collective result of every weird machine he'd been through. He'd sat down feeling like thirty minutes would seem like a year, but somehow, it had flown by.

He followed the nurse's directions into yet another bland office and sat down. A new doctor greeted him with a grim smile, the kind of smile that pulled Cam firmly out of his daydreams and into a harsh, uncompromising reality.

"The lump is a tumor," the doctor said without preamble. "Your preliminary diagnosis was almost certainly correct, and it looks like a classic germ cell seminoma. We've cautiously classified it as a T1 tumor."

"T1?"

"Stage one. From your test results, it doesn't appear to have spread."

"But it's still cancer, right?"

"Yes." The doctor turned his computer screen and pointed to an unintelligible, dark mass. "The tumor is here, on the left side. It's easily accessible and a common type for men your age. The best course of action is to remove it, and the surrounding tissue, and blast you with a course of radiotherapy. If that's successful, we may be able to avoid chemotherapy."

Tumors. Chemo. Cam's blood rushed in his ears. Someone was yanking his chain. They had to be. "How would you remove it?"

"We'd take the whole testicle."

"What? You wanna cut my balls off? Fuck, no!" Cam's heart thudded to a standstill. He stood. His chair tipped back and clattered to the floor.

The doctor raised his hand. The gesture was calm and placating, like the scene was a replay of something he'd seen a thousand times over. "It's not quite as brutal as that. The surgery is called an orchiectomy, and the diseased testicle is removed through an incision in the abdomen."

"No." Cam backed away from the doctor's desk. "There's nothing wrong with me. I feel just fine."

"And there's every chance you'll stay that way if you have the surgery and have it soon. As far as cancer diagnoses go, this is good news, Mr. Shaw. Very good news."

Cam stood very still. He'd known for the past week that this was at least a possibility, but that didn't make the images in his head any easier to bear. "What about..." He stopped. *What about my dick? Will it still work?* Was he really about to say that? Or was he going to say nothing and wait until he next dropped his pants on set and let the world know there was nothing there.

Fuck, what did you even call a man with no balls? Was he even still a man?

The doctor retrieved a card from a drawer and wrote something on it. "I'm sure you have a lot of questions, so I'm going to schedule an appointment with our psychotherapist. She's very experienced in this field, and a lot of my patients find her invaluable. She has a clinic this afternoon in the oncology wing. I'll give her a call and let her know you're coming."

Cam accepted the card and righted his chair in silence. The doctor made his calls, then produced a bunch of literature and proceeded to explain in excruciating detail how life as Cam knew it was about to implode.

After, he drifted out into the corridor, numb and almost detached from the chaos inside his own head. His phone vibrated in his pocket. He pulled it out and read the message from Jon.

Kai. Saturday 2 p.m.

Apathy swept over Cam. He walked three yards along the corridor and dropped his phone in the trash can.

It didn't take long to find the oncology wing. The building was neutral enough, but inside the scent of illness and death was strong, to Cam, at least. He made the mistake of looking up just once and, after that, kept his eyes on the shiny floor as he made his way to his eleventieth clinic of the day. He gave his name to another receptionist, who directed him to yet another hard, plastic chair.

He sat down and put his head in his shaking hands. The doctor had been encouraging…positive, almost. The surgery and subsequent biopsy would give a final, definitive diagnosis, but if his test results were accurate, his type of cancer had a 95 percent survival rate—survival and complete recovery.

He was lucky, he knew he was, but the roiling pit of dread in his belly wouldn't quit. Up until his lazy discovery, he hadn't felt the tumor at all, but now it was *all* he could feel…feel it eating him up from the inside out like the destructive intruder it was.

The doctor said he wasn't going to die, that he probably wouldn't even get that sick, but he felt sick now. Sick and tired. It had been a long day, and all he wanted was the solitary comfort of his bed. A sure sign that something wasn't right. He rarely craved his own company.

"Hey."

"Huh?" Cam raised his head, startled. He'd neither felt nor seen someone sitting in the chair beside him. He blinked, and his vision cleared to reveal a set of deep brown eyes he felt like he knew.

The brown eyes crinkled up at the sides as the tanned face they belonged to eased into a tentative smile. "Cam? It *is* you, right?"

Cam stared. Sasha's face was indelibly imprinted in his brain, but he'd thought of little beyond his own balls since the beginning of the week. He opened his mouth and shut it again. Words failed him.

Sasha frowned and touched his arm. "You okay?"

No. "What are you doing here?"

Sasha stole his warm gaze from Cam and took a glance around. "I might ask you the same thing. This *is* the clinic for young men with testicular cancer."

"You have cancer?"

"Not anymore. I just got my all clear. This is my last session with Dr. King."

"That's good. That's really good." Cam put his elbows on his knees. "You're not sick? You're okay?"

"I'm fine, Cam. Do you want some water?"

Cam waved the bottle away. "I'm good."

Sasha was silent a moment; then he put his hand on Cam's arm, squeezing when Cam didn't respond. "What are you doing here? Are you sick?"

"Apparently."

The single word was choked and hoarse, but it was enough for Sasha to change his posture…to move his chair closer to Cam and shift his hand up to Cam's shoulder.

Cam closed his eyes. It felt good, really good, like he could drift away to another world.

"Cam?"

Or not. Cam opened his eyes and realized Sasha was waiting for him to elaborate. "Germ cell seminoma. They want to cut it off."

Sasha nodded like the two clipped sentences spoke a thousand words. "When were you diagnosed?"

"Um." Cam checked his watch. "An hour ago?"

"And you're here by yourself?" Sasha raised an eyebrow, making his face seem wiser than his boyish features. "Where's your folks?"

"Haven't told them yet. The quack at the…fuck, I don't even know where. He told me to come here."

"To counseling? Makes sense. I didn't see Dr. King until after my surgery. Wish I'd manned up and come a lot sooner."

Cam took a shallow breath. With Sasha's warm, familiar presence beside him, the spinning room was coming back into focus. "Why are you here now, if you're not sick anymore?"

"Tying up loose ends. It's ironic, but the good news threw me for a loop. I didn't know what to do without a badass shadow on my shoulder. That's why I haven't called you. I've been kinda lost in my own head."

In spite of himself, Cam felt his natural, ingrained curiosity spike. "Do you know now? What to do, I mean?"

"Maybe. Ask me in a few weeks."

The receptionist called Cam's name. Dazed, he rose to follow her directions. Sasha caught his arm. "Wait. Call me later. Let me know you're all right."

Cam choked out a humorless bark of laughter. "I don't have a phone."

Sasha conjured a pen from nowhere and took hold of Cam's arm. "Don't wash this off, okay? Write it down and give me a call…anytime, dude. Just pick up the phone."

CHAPTER EIGHT

"Action!"

The command went over Cam's head. He hadn't seen Kai in a while, and his petite, flaxen-haired friend had been all over him the moment he'd stretched out on the bed beside him. It seemed they were starting their scene long before Jon saw fit to begin, and that suited Cam just fine. His head was fucked, and he needed this…needed the distraction of Kai and his smooth, pliant body. Kai was a little petite for his tastes, but he had a great smile and a subtle undertone of aggression that hadn't been there the last time they'd shot a scene together. The last time Cam had seen Kai get fucked on-screen was with Levi, and *no one* showed that side of themselves to Levi. Rex had tried and gotten his ass kicked across the set.

Cam rolled over, kissed Kai hard, and shoved his hand into Kai's curly blond hair. He tugged, enjoying the wide-eyed gasp Kai gave him in return.

Kai nipped at Cam's neck. "Hey. You're supposed to be the nice one."

"Who told you that?" Cam rose up and stripped his shirt.

Kai licked his lips and moved his hands straight to Cam's chest. "You did, when I first started dancing at the club."

Yep, that sounded like the kind of shit Cam spouted at the increasingly younger boys Jon recruited into his ranks. "What else did I say?"

"That you'd show me a good time. I've been waiting on this for months."

Makes two of us. Though, it wasn't Kai Cam had been waiting on. He'd just been…waiting.

He pulled Kai down the bed, undoing his fly with one hand. Kai was bare beneath his shorts and already hard. He bucked up into Cam's hand and let out a breathy gasp that went straight to Cam's own half hard dick.

Half-hard. Huh. That was new. Cam's cock was usually the first to the party, on set or anywhere else sex was on the table.

Kai reached for Cam's waistband. Cam rolled away, deflecting him for now. Blue Boy fans didn't go for flaccid cocks. They probably didn't appreciate condemned balls either, but Cam had checked himself from every angle, and though the tumor was all *he* could see, the camera wouldn't pick it up, and neither would anyone else.

He took Kai in his mouth, hoping the sensation of a warm, pulsating dick would stir his own. He loved giving head, on and offscreen, but it had been a while since he'd had the pleasure without a camera watching his every move. Jon didn't seem to enjoy it, or anything else Cam wanted to do to him. No. That heady street of torture was all one-way.

Damn it. Why was Cam thinking about Jon? Before the tumor, he'd shut that shit down.

Kai shuddered. "Fuck!"

Cam smiled to himself, knowing he'd put Kai right on the edge with just the tip of his tongue. He was damned good at head; even Levi, Mr. Stoic himself, said so. It took a little longer to get his own dick to play ball, but Kai had come a long way in the months since he'd shot his first scene at Blue Boy, and he'd learned a lot.

And once Cam was naked and hard and presented with Kai's willing, open body, his mind went blank.

He drove his fingers into Kai, twisting and stretching him, testing the preparations Kai had no doubt done before he'd come on set. It was something Cam always did, even if he knew the other model was more than ready. He had to feel it for himself, had to *know* whatever came next would be a pleasure for everyone involved.

He found no resistance in Kai, just heated, clenching flesh. Kai countered his hand, pressing himself ever closer. He wrapped his arms around Cam's neck and kissed him sweetly on the cheek. "Feels so good, baby."

Cam smiled and pushed Kai's fast-dampening hair out of his face. He was good at these scenes—the ones the recent influx of female fans requested all the time. Jon set them up to be almost like two lovers, boyfriends, having their own private moment, and the more emotional viewers lapped them up, imagining real-life relationships that didn't exist, and barraging Jon with requests for more.

Usually, it was kind of humorous—a running joke that bonded the cast and crew of Blue Boy together—but not today. For Cam, today wasn't about emotions, good or bad. This was about getting off, raw and empty, and chasing the burn of pleasure that would leave his mind devoid of all else.

The scene snowballed, and the routine of hands, mouth and tongue passed Cam by. A condom appeared on his dick, by his hand or Kai's, he wasn't quite sure. A haze descended over his vision. He rolled Kai onto his belly, squeezed his ass, and slammed into him. Kai took the impact and gripped the metal frame of the bed, the one with the deliberately loosened bolts.

On cue, the bed squeaked and groaned, entwining with the brutal snap of Cam's hips, Kai's gasps, and resonating around the set. Cam breathed it all in, grinding out a rhythm that grew in intensity with every thrust. Hard and fast. Sharp and sure, belying the forty-eight hours of insomnia he'd lived through to get to this point. His muscles burned with the effort, tense and sore, but his body responded to the tight heat of Kai clamped around him, wanting…craving more with each slam of his hips.

Kai whimpered. Cam faltered, and Kai's tight face came back into focus, his discomfort clear.

What the hell am I doing?

Cam dropped Kai and reared back, horrified. Kai was his friend, and Cam wasn't that kind of top…wasn't that guy who pounded the men beneath him into submission. His stomach rolled, and the queasy sensation he'd had in the pit of his stomach for days returned full force.

I need to get out of here.

Kai sat up and caught Cam's shoulders. He pushed him back on the bed and climbed over him. "Yeah, let me ride you."

He lowered himself onto Cam's cock before Cam could protest.

Startled, Cam arched his back and winced. Something felt off. It wasn't pain, but the weight on his groin felt all wrong. Kai pressed down on him over and over, but the feeling increased until Cam couldn't breathe through the pressure in his gut.

Kai dropped to his chest, his thin arms shielding Cam from the camera. "Are you okay?"

Fuck no. Cam met Kai's gaze, his response silent and still but loud enough to reach Kai's young ears all the same.

Kai circled his hips, watching Cam's face, gauging his reaction. He kept his movements slow and gentle at first, only upping the pace when Cam got a tenuous hold on himself and nodded.

Let's get this shit done.

Cam clenched his eyes shut and focused on Kai his lips and teeth on his neck. His ragged gasps and quivering thighs. The smooth heat of him wrapped around Cam's cock.

I can do this.

Cam sucked in a breath and opened his eyes. Kai studied him a moment, then leaned back, revealing Cam to the cameras again, and took him deeper into his body.

The angle change felt better…good, even. Some of the anxiety gripping Cam's chest faded. He wondered if his brief slip had been caught on-screen. One look at Jon's face would tell him, but he knew better than to search him out. Jon got real pissed when a shot caught models looking anywhere off set.

Kai pinched Cam's thighs. A faint hum of pleasure bloomed in Cam's belly. Encouraged, he widened his legs and took over the pace. Kai relaxed and threw back his head, groaning and pulling his own hair.

"Fuck, more."

Cam fucked him harder. Heat spread from his cock and into his veins. The black mist returned. Yes. He wanted this. He craved this. He pounded Kai faster, twisting his hips, and watched for the eye roll that told him he'd found the right spot.

Kai cried out and reached for his own dick. He fell forward, steadying himself on Cam's chest, and pumped himself at a brutal pace. "Gonna come."

Cam felt relieved. His mind was relinquishing control to the dizzying pleasure of being inside Kai, but his body was tired, and all at once, everything ached—like they'd been fucking for hours rather than minutes.

Kai came with a high-pitched gasp. His warm, sticky release hit Cam's chest. Cam watched his face contort, felt him shudder, and absorbed the sensation. He fucked him a few moments longer, then pulled out to finish himself off by hand.

For a minute that seemed to last a lifetime, his climax teased him, hovering just out of reach. Frustrated, he chased it down. Goddamn it. It was the only reason he'd showed his face at the studio at all. The only reason he'd left the pity party he'd created for himself on his couch.

He worked himself at a frenzied pace. Sweat beaded his chest, and heat flushed his face. He growled, squeezing himself a little too hard, but it was enough. Just. He came with no sound, an anticlimax in every sense of the word.

"Cut!"

Cam stood with his hands flat on the tiled wall, letting the hot water pummel his neck. He soaped up and washed away the sweat and grime of the scene. His arms felt weighted and tired, but the lump of death in his balls felt heavier, dragging him down, like he could sink through the floor at any moment.

"Sorry if I jumped on you a little too hard."

Cam glanced at Kai. He'd half forgotten he was there. "Huh?"

"That bit where your eyes watered. Sorry if I caught you in the balls. I've done that before. Sonny keeps telling me to keep my pointy knees to myself."

He thinks that was his fault? "Don't worry about it. I'm not…" Cam stopped and gathered his words. "It wasn't you, man. Don't sweat it. I'm not with it today. Thanks for covering for me. Most guys wouldn't have noticed."

Kai shrugged and shut off his shower. "Sonny told me I had to watch every guy I filmed with. Look them in the eye, you know? Even if it's just a fucking handjob. He said no one comes to the studio without bringing a slice of their day with them. Guess you're having a bad day, huh?"

Fucking Sonny. He's too young to be so wise. "Yeah, I guess."

Kai kissed his cheek and left him alone, disappearing into the depths of the studio. Cam was grateful for the peace. Kai was a good friend, sweet and caring, and though they'd never hooked up offscreen, Cam had often let Kai sleep in his bed with him after a

61

long night at Silver. He'd always gotten the feeling Kai didn't want to go home, and he wasn't about to argue with that. How could he? No one knew where Kai went when he wasn't at the club, the studio, or curled up like a lost puppy on someone's couch.

Cam finished up in the shower and got dressed, hoping to make a quick escape, but Jon caught him and pointed to his open office door. A summons, if ever Cam saw one.

"Lock the door."

Cam obeyed and leaned with his back against it, wondering what Jon had in mind. The ugly scene at the club seemed a lifetime ago, and they hadn't spoken since, but Cam recognized the gleam in his eye. "Do you need me for something?"

Jon pointed at his computer monitor. "Check this out."

Cam pushed off the door and rounded the desk to be greeted by a screenshot of himself, naked and jacking off over Kai's trembling form. Surprise coursed through him, though he wasn't sure why. It had been his reality twenty minutes ago. "You like it?"

"Hell, yeah." Jon pulled Cam into an embrace that would've appeared affectionate from anyone else. An embrace Cam couldn't bring himself to dodge. "I like watching you get off. I should get you to jack for me more often."

Cam rolled his eyes. Jon had a thing for watching him fly solo. "Was the scene good?"

"Mmm." Jon ground himself into Cam's back. "Very good. Did you enjoy it?"

No. "Yeah." Cam relaxed a little into Jon. The last few days had been lonely, and though he knew it wasn't meant as such, and however much Jon's arms weren't the arms he craved, being held felt comforting. "Kai's a good bottom."

"That he is." Jon's voice was distant and thoughtful as he popped the button on Cam's board shorts and slipped his hand inside. Cam hardened, despite his recent release. *Damn it, Jon.* Their emotional connection was nonexistent, but the sexual energy between them was undeniable.

"I've never fucked you in here." Jon pumped Cam slowly. "Would you like it if I fucked you right here over my desk."

"Probably."

Jon tightened his grip on Cam's cock, asserting the dominant authority Cam had grown unhealthily addicted to. "Pardon?"

"Yes." Cam fell forward, his hands flat on the desk, rolling his hips in time with Jon's languid rhythm.

Jon chuckled and opened a drawer. "You'd have to be quiet, Cam. Silent. Do you think you could do that?"

"Ye—*Shit*." Cam jolted, feeling cool lube drizzle into his ass. Yeah. He could do that. Clench his eyes shut, jam his fist in his mouth, and get fucked.

Jon's fingers brushed Cam's balls. Cam froze. Reality slammed back into perspective, and he pulled away. He didn't want this. Not now, not ever. He twisted out of Jon's grasp and shoved his cock back in his shorts.

Jon raised a silent, questioning eyebrow, unfazed by Cam's abrupt rejection. Almost like he'd expected it. "Problem?"

Cam caught his breath and shrugged. "I'm tired. I'm gonna split."

"That's all you have to say?"

"What do you want me to say? I'm not your fucking sex toy."

"Okay." Jon folded his arms across his chest. "If you don't want to do *this*"—Jon gestured between them—"that's fine. But you need to at least tell me what's up with the rest of your work."

"Excuse me?"

Jon beckoned him back to the computer and clicked a few buttons, bringing up the viewer comments posted under the various scenes on the Blue Boy site. "Look at this, and this, and this. What do you have to say about that?"

Cam squinted at the computer screen. The comments were small, but there were reams of them, all saying the same thing. *What's up with Cam? Where's Cam's big smile gone? Why is Cam so sad? What's up with Cam? What's up with Cam? What's up with Cam?*

Cam frowned, looking at the dates. They went back months. He couldn't even blame the cancer diagnosis for most of them. There was only one correlation that made any sense. The breakdown of his parents' marriage and the shoulder he'd found to cry on.

Sudden, white-hot anger surged through him. He shoved the computer monitor away, tipping it onto its side, enjoying the crash and the shock in Jon's face. "*That's* how you gauge my well-being? You have me tied up in your bed, and some faceless Internet geek jerking off has to tell you I'm not fucking happy? Fuck you!"

"Cam…"

Cam dodged Jon's outstretched hands and started for the door. He heard Jon behind him as he fumbled the lock, but when the door swung open, he knew Jon wouldn't follow.

CHAPTER NINE

Cam breathed deeply, letting the salty air fill his lungs and the morning sun warm his face. The sea breeze refreshed him, and his board felt good beneath his feet. The squeak of BMX brakes sounded beside him. He opened his eyes and grinned. Sasha winked and tore off ahead of him, riding like a demon until he slowed to slide along a deserted bench.

The grind trick was a little rusty, but it made Cam smile. He'd had a long week. Doctors' appointments, filling out insurance forms. Trying to figure out who to tell first. Getting sick was a ball ache. Literally. By Friday morning he'd had enough, and the evening had found him searching his pockets for the scrap of paper he'd scrawled Sasha's number on and trudging to the store to buy a prepaid phone.

And here they were, careering along the dawn-lit seafront the very next morning. They'd exchanged few words, but it didn't seem to matter. Sasha was calm and warm…and he *knew*. Knew the dark secret Cam had yet to share with another soul.

Cam put his foot to the ground. The scenery whizzed by until he caught up with Sasha a few feet away from the bench. He jumped it, skidding along the seat, and came to a sharp stop by Sasha's front tire.

Sasha eyed him. "You're pretty fast on that thing. Thought I'd be waiting on you all morning."

"Bite me." Cam showed Sasha his middle finger. "How far do you want to go?"

"As far as it takes."

Cam tilted his head to one side. "For what?"

"For you to tell me what you need."

Sasha shot off again without elaborating. Cam followed him, pondering his answer. Sasha had asked him on the phone if he wanted to talk. He'd said yes, but now he wasn't quite so sure. His misguided day at the studio had been a mistake, of that he was certain, but could he find the words to explain that to Sasha? Probably not.

He met Sasha by a food cart, ignored Sasha's proffered water bottle, and bought an icy blue drink that stained his tongue.

Sasha rolled his eyes. "You need to take better care of yourself than that."

"Why? Doesn't matter if my balls turn blue, does it?" Cam kicked his board into his hands and drifted to a nearby bench.

Sasha followed, pedaling with lazy legs. He dismounted and leaned his bike against the back of the bench. "I know you're smarter than that."

"Do you?"

"Hell, yeah. Radiotherapy's gonna kick your ass. It's not like chemo, but it ain't no joke. You need to be ready."

It was the first time either man had overtly mentioned the elephant hanging over them. Cam remembered Sasha's words in the hospital. *"…a badass shadow on my shoulder."*

Yeah, or in my freakin' boxers.

"Something funny?"

Cam crunched the ice in his drink. "Nope. Just being a dick."

"You're allowed for the time being, at least until after your surgery. Did you get a date?"

"Wednesday."

Cam threw his half-full cup in a nearby trash can. Sasha was easy to be around, but Cam didn't want to talk about this, even to someone who knew exactly how he felt. Talking about it made it real. Fuck that. He had four days left to pretend, and he was going to make them count.

"How are your folks taking it? Mine freaked. Think my mom took it worse than me."

"Um…" Cam averted his gaze, but Sasha interpreted his silence with widened eyes.

"You haven't told them? Cam, you can't do this on your own. What about your friends?"

"Nope."

"Why not?"

Cam shrugged. "Haven't found the right time. My parents divorced this year. It's been rough on my dad and my kid brothers. I don't want to put them through any more shit."

Sasha leaned back on the bench and stretched out his legs. Cam watched his calf muscles strain and relax. The dude had hot legs. Tanned and covered in fine, fair hair. The kind of legs Cam liked to bite and knead, given the right context.

"Dude, they'll be more upset if they find out after the fact. You're close to your folks, right? You've mentioned your dad a few times. You should tell them, and soon. Rip off that bandage."

Cam sighed. He felt more relaxed with Sasha, a virtual stranger, than he had in days…no, weeks, but no amount of eye fucking him could change his reality. "My sister's gonna lose her shit."

"That's what sisters are for." Sasha nudged his arm. "And maybe you need that. Denial only lasts so long."

Cam snorted. "I'm not in denial."

"Yeah? How do you feel right now?"

It was a trick question, and the psychologist in Cam knew the answer on the tip of his tongue was exactly what Sasha expected him to say.

He said it anyway. "I feel fine. Don't feel sick at all."

"And that's the problem." Sasha fired his empty water bottle into the trash can and retrieved his bike. "You only know you're sick because some quack told you so—"

"Three quacks."

Sasha grinned; then his face fell serious again. "I know it's the worst bit, in the beginning, at least. Eventually, radiation and chemo make you feel like hell, but even that doesn't last. Most of the time, you only know you're sick 'cause dudes in white coats keep telling you."

"You had chemo?"

"Twice." Sasha mounted his bike and checked his watch. "Come over to my place tomorrow. I'll cook you some real food and tell you all about it."

Cam climbed out of the cab and stared around him in disbelief. He took in the sweeping driveway and landscaped lawns and shook his head. This couldn't be right. He squinted at the crumpled scrap of paper in his hand, deciphering his own scrawl, and gazed again at the lavish surroundings, but nothing changed. If he was in the right place, Sasha Tate was a freakin' millionaire.

The taxi rolled away. Cam started up the driveway, feeling out of place with every step. Some people in porn flashed a lot of cash, but not like this. Sculpted gardens, security cameras, and electric gates? This was *real* money. Cam half expected a cop car to pull up beside him and arrest him for trespass.

"You found it, then?"

Cam spun around. Sasha stood behind him, perched on his ever-present BMX, his grin lazy, like he'd just woken up. Perhaps he had. Cam knew he had a penchant for afternoon naps. The thought was a balm to his churning insides. "Hard to miss. What are you, a prince or something?"

Sasha rolled his eyes and scratched his belly, revealing a sliver of his taut, tanned abdomen. "This is my parents' place. I rent the pool house. Come on, this way."

Cam followed Sasha up the driveway and around the back of the biggest house he'd ever seen up close. Tennis courts, plush outbuildings Sasha said were a gym and his father's sports car garage, and finally, a large, heated pool.

"This is me." Sasha pointed to a redbrick bungalow that opened out onto the poolside. "I'll show you."

The inside of the bungalow was sleek and stylish, furnished with modern decor and appliances, but it was lived in, with little touches of Sasha everywhere—bike parts, tools, weathered sneakers, and a stack of CDs on the coffee table. Cam liked it. "Nice place."

"Thanks." Sasha pointed to a stool at the breakfast counter, directing Cam to sit. "I moved back here when I got sick. Made things easier for my mom. She worried less, you know? I should probably get a place of my own again sometime, but my folks spend most of the year on the East Coast these days, so I'm here by myself a lot."

"Because you're better."

It wasn't a question, and Cam uttered the words to himself as much as Sasha, but Sasha nodded anyway. "Yeah, I'm better, Cam. Want a beer?"

"Hmm? No, thanks. I'm fine." Cam's gaze fell on a bubbling pot on the stove. "What are you cooking?"

Sasha placed a bottle of water on the countertop. "Chicken stew. Dumplings. Figured you could use some comfort food."

Cam absorbed the scent of chicken and herbs with muted interest. He hadn't been hungry in days. "Thought you'd make me eat some wheatgrass shit or something."

"Maybe next time."

Sasha messed around in the kitchen a little while longer. Cam watched him, enjoying the natural way he moved. He'd missed this—the easy banter and warmth—and it was almost enough to blot out the real reason Sasha had asked him to come. To forget that he was here for no other reason than Sasha felt sorry for him.

Cam cast his gaze around the bungalow's living space, searching for signs of Sasha's illness, though what he thought he'd find, he wasn't quite sure. His balls in a jar on a shelf, maybe?

Stop it.

Sasha's hand landed, firm and warm, on his shoulder. "Earth to Cam? Come on, dude. Let's eat."

Cam jolted back to reality. Somehow he'd missed Sasha loading bowls with food and carrying them past him to the coffee table. He followed Sasha to the big, squishy couch and sat, accepting the bowl Sasha shoved his way.

"Eat," Sasha said again, "then we'll talk. I promise."

Cam ate. The stew was good, though he lost interest long before he had the nerve to put his bowl down. Sasha watched him the whole time, his gaze shrewd. When he was done with his own food, he took both bowls to the kitchen and returned with two mugs of coffee.

Cam raised an eyebrow. "Thought you didn't do caffeine?"

"It's decaf, and I'm not a saint, you know. Or one of those nuts you see dressed in burlap at the health food store. I got into eating better when I was having chemo. I felt like crap for the best part of a year, and the little things helped."

"My doctor reckons I might not need chemo."

"That's good." Sasha took a sip from his mug and set it down. "That's really good. They musta caught it early. Mine was stage three by the time I started treatment."

Cam sat up, his curiosity roused despite the urge to stick his head in the sand. "Was your tumor really small?"

"No. I just didn't have the, um, balls to do anything about it. I knew it was there three months before I went to my doctor."

"Three months? Fuck. Did you know what it was?"

"I had a vague fear in the back of my mind, but mostly I was too embarrassed to walk into my doctor's office and drop my pants."

Cam chewed the inside of his mouth. Sasha's inhibitions seemed logical, in theory, but getting his cock out in front of people was second nature to Cam and, of this whole mess, was the least of his worries. "I couldn't stand it. I had to know. I went to my doctor the day after I found it."

"You did the right thing." Sasha nudged Cam with his elbow, reminding Cam he was just a heartbeat away from him on the couch. "I know it's scary as hell, but this could all be over in a few months."

"What happened after your diagnosis? Did you have surgery? What do your balls look like now?"

Sasha blinked at the sudden influx of questions, then raised the corner of his mouth in an ironic smile. "What if I told you I had none?"

"What?" Cam's stomach lurched, and he spluttered into his drink.

Sasha grinned. "I'm kidding, Cam. Calm the fuck down. I had my right one removed four years ago."

Cam glared, but weighed down with a bucketload of shameful relief, the effort was halfhearted. "What's it like? Does it look weird?"

"Not really." Sasha paused, his face thoughtful. "But it's different for me. I don't pay my bills with my junk. To be honest, I don't notice it much anymore. I'm only conscious of it in certain situations."

A click sounded in Cam's brain. His mind flashed briefly to the scene in the club, the kiss, the wandering hands. He figured he'd found the answer to Sasha's subtle shutdown, but something else caught his attention. "I don't pay my bills with porn, either. I have a regular job for that."

"So why do you do it?"

"At first, to pay for college, but I liked it, so I carried on. I give my dad some money from time to time, but I mostly leave the extra cash in the bank."

"What for? Saving up for something?"

"Not really." Cam swallowed a mouthful of tepid coffee. "It's just…there. Hey, can I ask you something?"

"Fire away."

"Were you scared?"

"Terrified," Sasha said without hesitation. "I heard the word 'cancer' and assumed I was gonna die. Then, when they told me it had spread, I figured it would be sooner rather than later."

"It spread?" Cam felt his heart slow to a sickening thud. The thought of a world without Sasha was unthinkable. "What happened next?"

"After my first surgery, they went back and took some lymph nodes from my belly. Then they blasted me with chemo until I felt pretty much dead anyway. Looked it too."

Cam stared, trying to imagine Sasha anything but the strong, tanned picture of health he was now. Couldn't do it. "When was this?"

"Three years ago. I was twenty-two when I was first diagnosed, but I've been cancer free for more than a year now. They think I'm done."

"That's good." Cam sank back on the couch, letting out a rush of air that made him feel somehow lighter. He knew there was far more to Sasha's story than he'd revealed so far, but the ending was clear—he was okay. He was alive. "What about your dick? Does it still work?"

Sasha rolled his eyes. "Dude, you're obsessed, but, yes, it works just fine. Don't think I'm all that fertile, but I guess that doesn't really matter."

They talked a little while longer, about cancer and beyond. Sasha's easy vibe had always made Cam feel good, and curled up on his couch, surrounded by all that was him, Cam couldn't help the wave of fatigue that washed over him. He hadn't slept well over the last few days…weeks, and the combination of a full belly and Sasha's comforting presence felt like he'd swallowed a sleeping pill. The light touches, the guiding hand on his arm. A friendship laced with a casual flirtation that didn't come at a price.

Cam's eyes drooped. Dazed, he considered going home, but Sasha's soft laugh and something heavy on his legs convinced him to stay.

It was dark when he woke up. Sasha was still beside him, but somehow in his sleep Cam had shifted closer than ever, slumping down with his head on Sasha's belly.

Sasha played with Cam's hair, watching him wake with amused eyes. "Okay?"

"Um, yeah. Shit. Sorry." Cam sat up, rubbing his face, and found himself inches from Sasha's lips. "Guess I was tired."

"Guess so." Sasha didn't move. He stared at Cam like it was the most normal thing in the world for them to be so entangled on his couch.

Cam's pulse quickened. Images of their first kiss filled his brain, but that wasn't what he wanted right now. Wasn't what he needed and craved. Sasha's breath was warm on his face, and he wanted to taste it, lose himself in it, and touch Sasha's lips with a kiss that felt like a gentle ocean breeze.

Their lips met, and it was everything he needed in that moment. The kiss was slow and soft and pulled Cam into a haze so sweet, he found his hands in Sasha's soft hair and his leg hooked over Sasha's hips before he knew he'd moved

Sasha cupped Cam's face in his rough, work-hardened hands and kissed Cam back, grounding him and holding him close.

Then he inhaled and pulled away, his face torn until his lips thinned to a determined line. He rolled off the couch and stepped back, putting a distance between them that felt like a fissuring chasm. "This can't happen."

Cam felt like he'd been punched in the gut. He'd taken Sasha's rejection before, but that didn't dull the burn of humiliation. "Sorry. Guess I just can't stop myself jumping on you."

"Don't be like that."

"Like what?" Cam forced himself up from the couch. "It's not like we haven't done this before. Where the fuck are my sneakers?"

"Cam…"

Cam dodged Sasha's outstretched arm. Somehow, he'd lost his shoes and the snapback ball cap he'd worn to keep his wayward hair in check. He spied the hat behind a sofa cushion and jammed it on his head. A wider sweep of the room found his sneakers by the back door.

He stomped over to them, but Sasha beat him to it, blocking his path.

"It's not what you think, okay? I don't want… Shit…" Sasha lost his words.

Cam laughed; he couldn't help it. "Dude, I get it. You don't want me. It's not that hard to understand."

"*That's* what you think this is? Me not wanting you? Goddamn it, Cam…" Sasha stopped again. His hands hovered, like he wanted to grab Cam and shake him. "This isn't about me. You might not know it, but you're not yourself at the moment. You don't *know* yourself, let alone what you really want."

Cam shook his head. He was tired and confused, but simmering beneath all that he was angry, real fucking angry. "Don't turn this around on me. I know what I want."

"Yeah? And what's that? You wanna bend me over the couch and fuck me until you can't remember what's tearing you up? Use your dick to make you feel better? 'Cause let me tell you, man, it won't work. Five minutes later, you'll be more miserable than when you fucking started."

Miserable. Cam turned the word over in his mind. It fit, so he kept it...held onto it and tried to smother it over the disproportionate fury choking him.

It didn't work. He couldn't breathe. He tried to open the door, desperate for fresh air.

Sasha blocked him again. "Cam, please—"

"Damn it, Sasha. Move!" Cam lashed out and drove his fist into the glass. It didn't break, but a crack formed and spread out, slow and creeping, like the icy dread Cam could feel in his bones. He hung his head and closed his eyes. "Just let me go, please?"

Silence, and then the dragging slide of the glass door as Sasha granted his wish. Cam opened his eyes and stepped out into the sunlight.

He walked away from Sasha without ever looking to see if the muffled sob he'd imagined was real.

CHAPTER TEN

Act(s)—kissing, blowing, fucking.
Partner(s)—Kai
Sick.
Lost.
Two words I can't shake. I've never felt like this before, like sex was so dirty and wrong. It wasn't Kai's fault, or even Jon and his cameras. It was mine. I shouldn't have been there. Porn suited me while I was drifting, not tied to anyone, not even myself. But not now. I'm different now, and it doesn't feel right. I feel like the porn gave me the cancer, like I brought it on myself, but I know that's not right either. Before…Jon, I loved it. It made me feel free.
Now, I feel like it's poisoned me from the inside out.

Cam stopped and put his pen down. His hand shook. He usually wrote more, but he'd been wrestling with his emotions for weeks, and seeing his darkest thoughts spelled out on paper scared him. His time with Sasha had calmed his sheer panic, but it seemed the effect was temporary. Or perhaps only existed in Sasha's presence. Alone in his apartment, Cam felt real, cold fear creep over him again. The kind of fear that made his chest hurt and his heart race.

The kind of fear that overcame even the disquiet from his fight with Sasha and the lingering embarrassment of rejection.

Cam shivered and glanced at the open bedroom window. It was Monday evening, two days before his scheduled surgery, and he hadn't heard from Sasha since he'd bolted from his cozy poolside bungalow the night before. And he wasn't sure he wanted to. After all, what else was left to say? Sasha had pulled away from him…twice, and after a long sleepless night, Cam figured he understood the message loud and clear.

I don't want you.

And he'd given up wondering why. Cancer, porn, and unfinished business with a possessive ex-lover, the specifics didn't matter. Put together, he wasn't exactly a catch.

Cam took a deep breath and stared hard at the ceiling. He'd been lying alone on his bed since he'd finished work at Beat Shak four hours ago. His day had been long and dull, concluding with a meeting with his boss to explain the leave of absence he needed to take for the surgery and subsequent treatment. The meeting was the first time he'd talked about the cancer with anyone who wasn't a doctor or Sasha. The short conversation had exhausted him, but despite that, he felt restless and keyed up, like he could climb out of his skin and claw his own eyes out. Sasha and the impending surgery kept him awake, but more than that, he couldn't stop thinking about porn, and the limitations he hadn't noticed it imposing on his life. His apartment was cold and lonely, *he* was lonely, and why? Because there was no one outside the studio he could call and confide in. Sonny was his friend, but he'd been MIA for weeks, and Cam couldn't face Levi's voice mail again.

But he couldn't spend another minute kicking around his apartment. The doctors had told him to rest up before surgery, take it easy and relax, but instead, Cam was driving himself crazy. He wasn't used to spending so much time by himself. This time last year, he'd had a place full of people, drinks flowing, temperatures rising, and perhaps that was part of the problem. Perhaps he'd been alone all along.

Cam rolled from his bed, giving himself a slight head rush, and moved to his closet. He'd ditched his Beat Shak T-shirt as soon as he'd come home, knowing he wouldn't need it for a while, and he'd been shirtless since then, intent on crashing out in bed and hiding under his duvet until the day of his surgery dawned. But it wasn't going to happen. There was something he needed to do, and he needed to do it *now*.

Thirty minutes later, he strolled past security at Silver as if he didn't have a care in the world. He bypassed the dance floor and made his way to the crowded bar. Silver was kicking, even on a Monday night, but Bull, Silver's resident manager, saw him and pointed to the backlit refrigerators. As a resident model, Cam had the right to help himself.

He took a cold bottle of beer and chugged half of it down in one long gulp. The rest slid down just as easy, *too* easy. He took another and continued on his way, downstairs to the staff-only basement of the club.

Jon's office was empty when he punched in the code to open the door. Cam wasn't surprised. Jon checked in at Silver every evening, but never before midnight. Cam glanced around, looking for a suitable medium for his leave of absence notice. A pen and paper didn't seem to cut it.

He rounded the desk and flicked on the computer. It usually took a few minutes to boot up, so Cam was surprised when the screen flashed to life almost instantly, and shocked when the image on-screen registered with his convoluted consciousness.

What the fuck?

Cam froze. He'd seen himself on-screen more times than he cared to remember. Watched his own scenes for pleasure. But he'd never seen himself depicted the way he was now. Tied up and begging. Head down, ass raised. Jon's to do with whatever he pleased. Cam leaned closer, clicked a few buttons. More images of his private moments with Jon lit up the screen. Jon's bedroom, Jon's couch. The wide, flat coffee table. Even the harsh words they'd exchanged at the studio after the scene with Kai were saved as an MP4.

Cam clicked on the thumbnail, turned the sound up, and watched himself let Jon back him into a corner, shove his hand down Cam's pants, and almost talk him into getting fucked right over the desk. Performing for a camera he hadn't known existed.

Ironic nausea rolled in Cam's belly. He opened the liquor cabinet and reached for a bottle. He took a robotic swig. Expensive whiskey burned his throat but did nothing to calm the horror building in his gut. Having sex with an audience was second nature, something he enjoyed when his life wasn't imploding, but this? Cam read the titles, and his tongue stuck to the roof of his mouth. He opened a document and read the eleven words that described the project for which he'd become an unwitting star.

Bound and Begging. Cam Carter as you've never seen him before…

Cam clicked on a few more links and files. He didn't know much about distribution, but the electronic paper trail was clear. Every sexual encounter Cam and Jon had ever had was edited to remove any identifying sign of Jon, polished, and ready to be loaded to the Blue Boy website.

Numb, Cam made a grab for the desk phone and jammed his finger on the Zero button, knowing it dialed Jon's personal cell. The cell he never turned off, even in bed…in bed with Cam.

Jon answered on the third ring. "Who's in my office?"

"Who do you think?"

Silence. Then, "Cam?"

"Had to think about that, didn't you? How many people know the code?"

"That's why you're calling?" Jon's condescending amusement washed over Cam like acid. "I know you can think of a better reason to be in my office than that."

"How about getting a preview of your new project? *Bound and Begging*. Sounds like pretty interesting viewing."

The pause at the other end of the line was barely detectable, but to Cam, it was deafening.

"Do I want to know why you're going through my personal files?"

"Personal?" Red-hot anger flushed Cam's face. He felt like he was burning for all the wrong reasons. "There's nothing *personal* about putting this shit online."

"Says who? You've never had a problem with it before. Something you want to tell me?"

"Like what? Like I didn't consent to having my private sex life sold to line your pockets? Fuck you, Jon."

Jon sighed. "Really, Cam? You're going to play coy with me now? Nothing we do at Blue Boy is private. It's business…art, and I know you love it. Admit it. Being with me showed you a side of yourself you didn't know was there. Self-discovery. That's what you're all about, isn't it?"

Cam swallowed bile. Part of him wanted to argue, but the devil on his shoulder knew Jon's words were laced with truth. Bottoming, submitting, giving up control. He *had* loved it. He thought of Sasha, his big hands, strong arms, and muscled legs. Would love it again. Just not with Jon. Not anymore.

"It's not art if both parties don't consent, you sick fuck. It's just you being a motherfucking pervert."

Cam slammed the phone down without waiting for Jon's reply. With shaking hands, he returned to the computer and clicked through to the control panel. He wiped the hard drive, swallowing several more mouthfuls of fiery whiskey while he waited for the process to complete.

Then he unplugged the machine and pulled it apart with his bare hands for good measure. He poured what remained of the whiskey bottle over the twisted mass of metal and wire. Considered lighting the whole damned lot on fire.

The pounding bass of the dance floor above brought him to his senses.

Horrified, Cam lurched away from the desk. His breath caught in his chest. He needed to get out. *Now*.

He stumbled to the door and slipped out into the murky corridor. Silver was packed, hot and heady. Around him, half-naked bodies stood pressed up against the walls, kissing, clutching, squeezing. More. Cam pushed past them, ignoring the voices that shouted his name. Dodging the hands that reached for him.

Jesus. Was this what he'd become? A commodity? Nothing more than a product of the Blue Boy brand? Nothing more than a pawn in Jon's game?

Cam made it into the main area of the club. The crowds closed in around him. Beyond the dance floor he could see the exit. It was twenty feet away, but the distance felt like a mile. His blood roared in his ears. Sweat dripped down his back. The lights, the noise. The bellyful of liquor on an empty stomach. His vision narrowed, and it all came crashing down, closing in on him until he could no longer breathe. Couldn't see. Couldn't think.

He stumbled again, bumping shoulders with someone hard enough to leave a bruise. He closed his eyes, waiting for the impact of the hard, sticky floor.

It never came. Strong hands caught him. Cam opened his eyes to meet a familiar hazel gaze he'd missed more than he'd dared to admit.

Sonny held Cam's face, his eyes wide. "Cam? What's wrong?"

CHAPTER ELEVEN

Sonny kicked open the fire doors and pulled Cam outside. Cam blinked. He hadn't thought of that. A little way down the street, away from the buzz of the club, Sonny sat him on the curb. "I need to get my stuff. Stay here."

Cam sat. Despite his anxiety to escape the club, he'd run out of energy. It seemed like no time at all before Sonny was back. Sonny hauled Cam to his feet. He was half the size of Cam but looks were deceptive; Sonny was strong. Cam stumbled. Sonny caught him and steadied him with his arms around Cam's waist. "Whoa. You're wasted, dude. What's the occasion?"

Cam laughed, the sound so dark and bitter it surprised even him. "I'm not celebrating."

Sonny eyed Cam a moment, looking up at him, still holding him by the waist. From a distance, they probably looked like lovers. "You look lost."

"Maybe I am."

"You're definitely drunk." Sonny stretched up and kissed his cheek. "Come on; let's walk home."

Cam let himself be tugged toward Sonny's part of town with little complaint. He was tired, and it wouldn't be the first time he'd crawled back to Sonny's place after a wild night at Silver. "What time is it?"

"Just after twelve. I haven't even gone onstage yet. Jon's gonna fire my ass."

"No, he won't." It was true. Like Cam, Sonny was a commodity, but it would take more than a few missed shows for Jon to fire Sonny. Sonny was the hottest dancer in the city. Jon wouldn't let another club snap him up, and a few no-shows was probably good publicity, fueling a buzz with the crowds of fans who flocked to Silver to see the Blue Boy models up close.

Still, it was early, for Sonny, at least. "You don't have to come with me. I should go home."

"And miss you falling over your own feet?" Sonny squeezed Cam's hand—the hand he'd yet to release—and bumped his shoulder. "No chance. You're coming home with me. We haven't seen you for ages."

"We? Is Levi at your place?" Cam came to an abrupt stop, fulfilling Sonny's prophecy and tripping over his feet.

Sonny kept walking, yanking on Cam until he complied. "No. He doesn't like my place, he spends all his time tidying up, but I have a key to his apartment. Plus, I gotta bottle of back-shelf vodka in my bag, and I know the best way to wake him up."

Cam wasn't so sure. For a porn star—*ex*-porn star—Levi was pretty tame. Even back in his day, he hadn't partied much, preferring to duck out early and hit the sack. Besides, if he'd read the glint in Sonny's eyes right, the kind of awakening he had in mind was best done by himself. It had been a long time since Cam had last fooled around with Levi. He wasn't sure how the big man would react if Sonny jumped on his bed with Cam in tow.

But it turned out not to matter. Levi was awake when Sonny let himself into his apartment, lounging on the couch, beer bottle in hand, and he seemed pretty pleased to see Sonny.

Cam hovered in the doorway. Levi caught his gaze over Sonny's shoulder, his expression inscrutable, and Cam felt himself withdraw into the troubled darkness he'd come out to escape. Levi's place was familiar. He'd spent many nights here, taking advantage of Levi's skill in the kitchen and putting the world to rights over a crate of beer, but without Levi's usual warm welcome, it felt all wrong.

Levi appeared in front of him. Cam hadn't noticed him move, nor Sonny disappear. Levi put his hands on Cam's shoulders. "What's up?"

Cam shrugged. His mind was weighed down by a plethora of bullshit. He couldn't find the words to begin explaining it.

Levi pulled him into a light, platonic hug. "It's good to see you, man."

The embrace felt good. Safe. Cam pressed his face into Levi's shoulder. His anger-laced whiskey buzz was beginning to wear off. "It's good to see you too. I've been calling you."

"Really?" Levi released him with a clap on the back. "I changed my cell. Did Sonny give you my new number?"

"Aw, shit, I forgot." Sonny jumped over the back of the couch, dressed in nothing but the shiny underwear he was supposed to have danced in. "I figured we could just call you, but your cell keeps going to voice mail."

"I, uh, lost it." Cam averted his gaze. He'd yet to contact the phone company and tell them he'd "misplaced" his phone. Maybe he'd do it after the surgery.

"Lost it?" Sonny poured three shots of vodka over ice and beckoned Cam and Levi to the couch. "Not trying to avoid someone, are you?"

Cam trailed Levi to the big leather sofa, waiting for him to slouch down beside Sonny before he took his place at the opposite end of the couch. It felt a little strange to see Levi and Sonny so comfortable together. He'd worked, partied, and fooled around with them both, but somehow never at the same time. Having them all in one place felt weird. Good but weird. "Who would I be hiding from?"

"Jon?" Sonny's gaze was steady, but despite his constant chatter, his eyes were pink and tired, like he hadn't slept much over the weekend, though Cam imagined his own face looked much the same. "I saw you come out of the office at the club like a bat out of hell."

Cam snagged a shot of vodka and chugged it down. "I'm not seeing Jon anymore."

Sasha aside, it was the first time he admitted there was something between him and Jon to anyone, but Levi's expression didn't change at all, and Sonny's only reaction was to dump his feet in Cam's lap. Cam rubbed his thumbs on Sonny's muscled calves. The gesture was absent…natural, until he remembered Levi. He chanced a glance at Levi now, wondering if he'd react. He didn't.

"Is that what's been bothering you?" Sonny said. "How serious was it? I can't imagine you with someone like him."

Cam considered his answer. He'd never perceived his encounters with Jon as anything more than some crazily intense sex, but his throat still burned from his discovery in Jon's office. He didn't feel hurt; he felt…sick. "Don't imagine it. You won't like it."

"Then tell me…us. Talk about it, Cam. Putting shit in boxes doesn't work for you. Don't let it eat you up."

Sonny knew him well, and combined with his instinctive understanding of how his mind worked, Cam knew he couldn't hide from him. And perhaps he didn't want to anymore. "You won't like it."

The repetition caught Levi's attention. He shifted on the couch, not seeming to notice Sonny crawl into Cam's lap. "What the hell did he do to you?"

Cam swallowed, hiding his face in Sonny's neck for a moment. Could he do it? Could he really tell them that his own stupidity had allowed Jon to take advantage of him? That he'd become so distracted by sex he hadn't even noticed? With Sonny playing with his hair, maybe he could.

Sonny and Levi listened in silence as Cam made his confession. He told them everything, from the submissive sex games to the hidden cameras.

Levi's frown grew with every word. When Cam was done, he swallowed a shot of vodka, the last of the bottle. Somehow, they'd polished it off while Cam had been talking.

"I don't get it," Levi said. "That some kinda BDSM shit? I didn't know you were into that."

Cam shrugged. "Neither did I. It was good, though, for a while, at least."

"When did you start seeing Jon?"

"Summer sometime." Cam thought back. "I went to his Fourth of July party."

Cam let the sentence hang. Sonny shifted and pressed a soft kiss to his neck. "I get it. You were freaking out about your mom, so letting Jon make decisions for you comforted you. Submission is like that sometimes, an escape."

"You think I discovered a new kink and used it as an avoidance tactic?"

"Maybe."

It was an interesting theory, but Cam was past caring, and part of him was resigned to the fact that he'd probably never understand what had driven him into his warped relationship with Jon. Admitting his stupidity to his friends was more embarrassing than traumatic. Secret cameras aside, it wasn't like Jon had ever forced him into anything. He'd enjoyed the sex. It was the rest of it that left a bad taste in his mouth.

Levi's frown deepened. "I don't get it. What happened to your mom?"

"She left."

"Huh? Left? As in, broke up with your dad?"

Sonny raised his head and slanted a glance at Levi. Cam couldn't see his expression. "Didn't you know?"

"Nope. I had no fucking idea. When did this happen?"

Cam let out an ironic chuckle. "July third."

"Why didn't you tell me?" Levi shook his head. He could be hard to read, but Cam could tell he was shocked.

Cam shrugged. "It seemed tame compared to what your momma was putting you through."

"So? Doesn't mean I don't give a shit."

Cam sighed. "I know you do; it's just this mess with Jon. I knew you didn't like him, even before…Rex, and I kinda found myself caught up with him before I knew what I was doing, you know? And by then, I couldn't seem to tell anyone."

"You told me about your mom, but you never said a word about Jon," Sonny said. His tone was contemplative, though he didn't seem pissed.

Cam looked down at the patterns Sonny was tracing on his chest through the thin cotton of his T-shirt. "You didn't ask."

"Bullshit. I asked you about Jon last time I saw you. You blew me off."

Cam smirked at Sonny's choice of words. The extra vodka was seeping into his bones and making his head swim. "You've never complained before."

But his grin died when Sonny scowled. "See? That's what you've been doing ever since Jon got his hooks into you. Being all evasive and shit. We used to talk about everything. Now you don't talk to anyone."

Cam's humor sobered as he considered Sonny's theory. And his stomach dropped as he realized Sonny was right. Ever since his mom had decided raising a family was too much for her, he'd spent most of his time working, partying, or fucking. Or all three combined. But as he'd come to realize over the last few weeks, those pursuits had left him pretty damned lonely. The only exception was Sasha.

Cam's chest ached.

"Hey." Levi's hand was warm on his shoulder. "You wiped the hard drive, right? That mess with Jon is over now. Don't think on it no more."

Cam nodded and closed his eyes. Levi was closer than he thought, and combined with Sonny wriggling on his lap, the warmth from Levi's solid body felt reassuring.

Sonny let out a mellow laugh. "Give him a kiss, Levi. That'll cheer him up."

Cam peeled an eye open. "Levi doesn't kiss."

Sonny's grin was smug. "He kisses me."

"Really?" Cam eyed Levi, who looked amused. "Thought kissing was for schmucks?"

"What can I say?" Levi shrugged, unruffled. "Sonny broke me."

Sonny hissed through his teeth. "You didn't take much persuading."

Cam absorbed the smoldering glance Levi sent Sonny's way with conflicting emotions. The obvious affection between his friends warmed his heart, but beneath it all, he was jealous. He wanted it for himself, not from them, but from Sasha. And worse, he knew it had been his for the taking before Jon Kellar and his porn empire got in the way. "I was seeing someone else for a while."

"The hot blond you brought to the club?"

Cam cut his eyes at Levi. "How the hell do *you* know about that?"

Levi pointed at Sonny.

Sonny shot Cam a look that made him squirm. "Kai told me. Did you really think you could take him to Silver and keep it quiet?"

Cam had no answer, because Sonny was right. Taking Sasha to Silver had been fucking ridiculous, doomed from the start. The scene with Jon had just been the icing on the cake. "Doesn't matter now. He wants to be *friends*."

Cam's sigh was heavy, but Sonny smirked and gripped the hem of Cam's T-shirt. "Aw, don't look so sad. Friends can be good."

Despite his heavy mood, the gleam in Sonny's eye was tempting. Cam met Levi's gaze as Sonny relieved him of his shirt. "Are we cool?"

Levi's grin was soft and blurred by the empty bottle of vodka on the coffee table. "We're cool, man. Just don't leave me out."

Cam's reply was muffled by Sonny's lips on his. Cam's body responded to the kiss like an old friend. Used to Sonny's dominant inclination, Cam fell pliant beneath him and let himself be pushed and pulled until his back collided with Levi's bare chest.

Levi wrapped his arms around him, wove his fingers into Cam's hair, and tugged his head aside to expose his neck. He nipped the soft flesh. Cam shivered. They'd played this game before, more times than he cared to admit, but on Levi's couch with Sonny kissing a path down his belly, somehow it felt more…intimate? Cam was too drunk to find the right word.

Cam lay back and let his eyes fall closed. Let his strained muscles relax, one by one. Despite Levi's words it was clear they'd somehow decided between them that Cam was the center of their affections. Not that Cam was complaining. A Levi-Sonny sandwich?

Yeah. He could lose himself in that.

Clothes disappeared like they'd never been there at all. Cam didn't have to look to see Sonny's back arch and his graceful neck flare. To see Levi's strong arms ripple and pop. Cam writhed and shuddered. Absorbed it. Drank it all in through his tired bones. He felt Sonny's dick on his thigh, and Levi's hard at his back, and wondered idly how things were going to go down. He'd fucked Sonny many times over, and it was always good, but the thought of Levi inside him was thrilling. Levi was *big*. Perhaps bending over for him would make him forget…

Sonny blew warm air over Cam's balls. Cam jumped. For the first time in days, the poisonous intruder in his body had been the last thing on his mind.

He sat up, feeling Levi follow him, still molded to his back, and watched his dick disappear into Sonny's mouth. Even from the safety of Levi's arms, he could see the tumor bulging to the left of Sonny's stubbled jaw. Bold and crass. *Huge.* How could Sonny not see it?

Sonny flicked his tongue over the tip of Cam's cock. Cam moaned. Distracting pleasure surged through him, and he dug his teeth into Levi's forearm.

Levi rumbled in Cam's ear. "You like that?"

Cam arched his neck and searched out Levi's earlobe, sucking it into his mouth, enjoying Levi's low growl. "Fuck, yeah."

Sonny hummed, staring up at them and watching them interact as he swallowed Cam whole. Cam gasped. He'd taught Sonny the art of deep throating himself, and he'd taught him well. He broke away from Levi with a breathy grunt and fought to keep himself on the couch. Sonny's attention felt good, almost too good, like a guilty pleasure of the best kind.

The first, faint flickers of release tickled Cam's belly. He was a sucker for good head, and it had been a while since anyone with real skills had gone to town on him. And Sonny didn't hold back. His rhythm was sure and steady, and when Cam began to lock up and shake, Sonny let his fingers wander, tracing Cam's oversensitive balls and lower, brushing over Cam's ass like a ghost.

Frustrated, Cam ground himself down onto Sonny's fingers, chasing friction and the addictive burn of being breached.

Sonny released Cam's dick from his mouth, his gaze telling Cam he knew exactly what he wanted. "You sure?"

"Do it." Cam squirmed, unable to keep still. "Do it hard."

Sonny ignored him and sucked his index finger into his mouth, putting on a show that made Cam's toes curl.

Levi chuckled in Cam's ear, low and deep. "Don't watch him do that. He knows it drives me fucking crazy."

Cam tried to smile, but he was too far gone, lost in the haze of vodka-fueled lust. He moaned and opened his legs, licking his dry lips. Sonny took the hint and eased his finger into Cam's ass.

The burn was light and sweet. Cam craved something deeper, but his subconscious pleaded with him to relax and trust Sonny to guide him. He tried to listen and was rewarded with the devilish twist of Sonny's single finger and a blunt nail scraping the bundle of nerves hidden inside him.

Sonny took Cam into his mouth again, sucking him hard, countering the gentle sweep of his finger. The sensation was immediate and overwhelming. Cam's body clamped down on Sonny, and he came with a throaty cry.

His mind went blank. His head spun, and he thought he might faint. The blackness felt fucking amazing, but brief. Too brief.

A noise escaped him, a desperate, plaintive sound.

Levi stroked his damp hair away from his face, soothing him like he had a fever. "Easy now."

Cam fought for breath and focused on Sonny, watching him as he climbed over Cam's body for a kiss before stretching up to find Levi. Cam listened to them kiss, absorbing their growing moans and tiny gasps of air, but he didn't look up. Though Levi still held him tight and Sonny held his hand over Cam's thudding heart, watching them *kiss* felt wrong, like he was intruding on a private moment. Instead he let the rush of his fading orgasm carry him until his stomach lurched in protest of a night on the booze with no food to sustain it.

Cam wriggled from the couch and excused himself to the bathroom. Levi and Sonny didn't seem to notice him go, but when he came back a little while later, his belly purged of beer and hard liquor, Sonny was dressed in sleep pants and chucking pillows on the opened-out sofa bed. Aside from the smell of sweat and sex in the air, there was no sign of the sweetly frenzied three-way.

"Levi's too sober for an orgy," Sonny said by way of explanation. "He thinks we should have a slumber party instead."

Levi snorted and punched his arm, still in the boxers he'd never gotten around to shucking. "Shut your mouth. I could watch Cam fuck you all night, but it's not what he needs." Levi turned his shrewd gaze on Cam. "Don't look for answers in sex. They ain't there for you no more."

"Or at least call your mystery dude up and invite him," Sonny quipped, though his crazy energy seemed to have faded while Cam had been blowing chunks in the bathroom.

Cam sat on the arm of the couch, watching Levi lunge for Sonny and pin him to the bed with one arm. In his heart, he knew Levi was right, and the underlying message caught him off guard. He'd sought comfort from Jon in the worst way, and where had it got him?

Playing third wheel to his two best friends.

Sonny tugged on his arm. "Wanna be Levi's little spoon? He'll keep you warm."

Cam hesitated, wondering if he should just go home. Then Levi held out his hand. "Come on, dude. There's plenty of room."

Cam let himself be pulled from the arm of the sofa. He landed in a clumsy heap by Levi. Sonny laughed and set about arranging them all the way he saw fit—Cam with his back to Levi, and his face buried in Sonny's chest. Cam didn't fight it or even protest. He knew he was in the wrong place, but knowing his friends were wrapped around him, hands clasped and sharing quiet, loving kisses, somehow, he fell asleep.

CHAPTER TWELVE

Cam woke at dawn. His head was on Levi's chest. He looked for Sonny and found they'd scooted around in the night. At some point, Sonny had climbed over him and sandwiched Levi between them, both of them using the big man as a pillow, protected by his strong arms.

Tiny Kai aside, it had been a long time since Cam had woken up with someone. Dribbling on Sasha didn't count. When he spent the night with Sonny, they usually partied all night, fooling around and murdering songs on Sonny's beat-up guitar, and he'd never slept with Jon.

He peeled his cheek from Levi's chest and found Levi awake, watching him a wry grin.

Cam took a moment to focus. "Hey."

"Hey." Levi lifted his arm so Cam could move. "Sleep all right?"

Cam stretched, noting he was the only one still naked. "Yeah."

It was mostly true. He'd woken a few times, convinced he could hear Sonny and Levi fucking, but when he opened his eyes in the darkness he'd seen Levi on his back with his legs wrapped around Sonny, and he knew that couldn't be right.

Levi maneuvered himself from beneath a sound-asleep Sonny, covered him with a blanket, and pointed at the kitchen. "Go get cleaned up. I'll make breakfast."

Cam wasn't hungry, but he needed a shower. He accepted the sweatpants Levi tossed his way, and drifted to the bathroom. The shower cleared his head. It felt good to tuck his damp, wayward hair behind his ears, and the smell of whatever Levi was cooking made him feel even better.

Cam dropped onto a kitchen stool and slumped on the breakfast bar, poking idly at his crappy prepay phone. The phone that never fucking rang.

Levi slid him a glass of orange juice. "Expecting a call?"

"No." Cam pocketed the phone.

Levi grinned and punched his shoulder. "Bet you're glad we didn't have a fuckin' orgy last night now, huh?"

Cam looked up at Levi, took in his broad bare chest and gentle grin. "Yes and no. You were right, but…"

Levi nudged him again. "If we were meant to roll in the hay together, it'll happen. Get the rest of your life in order first."

Levi dropped his words of wisdom and returned to his spicy skillet. Cam watched him cook for a while. Onions, peppers, mushrooms. Eggs, potatoes, and cheese. If Cam put all that in a pan, he'd end up with a hot mess. Not Levi. Everything he cooked tasted like magic.

"Sonny still asleep?"

"Hmm?" Levi glanced over his shoulder, and his smiled faded. It was subtle, but Cam saw it all the same. "Think he's been up all damned weekend. I wonder how he functions sometimes."

That sounded like Sonny. "You know how he functions though, right?"

A shadow passed over Levi's face. "I've got an idea, but enough about Sonny. When are you gonna tell me all the shit you left out last night?"

"Meaning?"

Levi flipped spicy hash onto three plates. He covered the third and set it aside. "Listen, I know I'm not a fucking psych expert like the rest of you, but I'm not as dumb as you think."

"I don't think you're dumb."

"That's sweet." Levi slid a plate across the countertop. "But I still don't get it. Jon did a number on you, but there's more to this than him. Dude, you're like…inside out. What's done that to you?"

Levi was smiling, but his words hit home. The bullshit with Jon, the booze, fooling around with his friends. None of it was anything more than a distraction, and in the hungover haze of the early morning, Cam lost the will to hide. He stood, walked around the breakfast bar, and pushed his borrowed sweatpants over his hips.

Levi raised an eyebrow. "Hey, now. I thought we understood each other."

Cam ignored him and lifted his flaccid cock away from his balls. "What can you see?"

"Huh?"

"Give me your hand." Cam grabbed Levi's wrist. "Can you feel that?"

Levi stared at him like he'd grown two heads, but didn't resist as Cam guided his hand to the left side of his sac. For a long moment, Levi's expression remained the same, but Cam saw his eyes widen when he felt the hard, misshapen intruder.

"What the fuck is that?"

Cam stepped back, heat flushing his face, and tucked himself back into Levi's sweatpants. "A seminoma."

"A what?"

"A tumor." Cam dropped back into his seat, his appetite and tentative resolve gone.

Levi opened his mouth. Shut it again. "Is it…"

"Cancer? Yeah, they think so. They'll know for sure when they take it off, but they seem pretty certain."

Levi swallowed, then turned his back on Cam, washed his hands, and reached for the kettle. The silence seemed endless, punctuated only by the hiss and swoosh of water as Levi poured it into two mugs.

95

Cam slumped forward again and put his head on his arms. He let his eyes droop. Levi's hand on his shoulder startled him.

"What happens now?"

"They cut it off, analyze it, and decide if I need chemo. The way it stands now, they reckon I might get away with a blast of radiation."

"Cut it off?" Levi looked a little green.

"Yep, they're gonna take the whole thing, ball and all. I'm gonna be lopsided for the rest of my life."

"But the tumor will be gone." Levi let his hand drop from Cam's shoulder. He seemed to have forgotten it was there. "And that's good about the chemo, right? If you don't need it?"

"I guess. They don't know that for sure, though." Cam reached for one of the mugs Levi had dumped on the counter. It looked like tea, in a weird, gray sort of way. He took a sip and cringed. "What the hell kind of tea is that?"

Levi shook his head. "I have no idea. You kinda threw me a curveball. I was trying to be nice."

"Sorry."

"What?" Levi looked startled. "Aw, hell no, Cam. I'm the one who should be sorry. You've been going through all this shit, and I never fuckin' noticed. And for what it's worth, I *am* sorry. You've always been there for me. I shoulda been there for you."

Cam let it go. He was as guilty as Levi for letting the drama at the studio get between them, but he didn't feel like arguing.

"Does Jon know?"

Cam shook his head. "No. Apart from my boss at Beat Shak, you're the first person I've told." *And Sasha.*

"Not easy, is it? Telling people the bad stuff." Levi's gaze clouded, and Cam remembered his face when he'd let slip about his momma's death. Flat, distant, empty, but beneath the forced apathy, the pain had glittered like a snake in the grass. "When's your surgery?"

Cam blinked. *Fuck.* "Tomorrow."

"Tomo—what? Why so soon?"

Cam shrugged. "This kind of tumor grows real fast, and it's not that soon. I've known about it for a week or so."

"Are you ready?"

Am I? Cam considered the question, and reality crashed into him. He wasn't ready…not even halfway there. He hadn't told his dad, his sister…Sonny. "I need to go."

Levi caught him as he rolled off his stool. "Easy. Eat your breakfast first."

Cam shook his head. He needed to go, now, or he'd lose his nerve. "I need to see my dad."

"Cam." Levi stared at him like he wanted to say so much more. Then he reached for his keys. "Come on. I'll drive you."

The ride to his dad's place was silent. Levi wasn't much of a talker at the best of times, and Cam knew he'd shocked him. Cam stared out of the window, watching the familiar scenery fly by. He felt odd…detached somehow from his mind. When Wade's house appeared in his line of sight, it seemed almost surreal.

Levi shook him. "You awake?"

Cam stared at him. Of course he was fucking awake. Did Levi think he could sleep with his freakin' eyes open? "I'm cool."

He made no move to get out of Levi's truck. It was seven a.m. on a Tuesday morning. Wade would be stomping around, throwing paper-wrapped lunches and backpacks at his brothers before he set off for a long day at the truck yard. Did Cam really want to drop this on him now?

Levi read his mind. "You're out of time, dude. Just tell him. He's your family. He'll understand."

How Levi knew that, Cam would never know. Levi was all alone in the world, and he had been long before his crazy momma took a walk in front of a truck. "What about Sonny? I need to tell him."

"Don't worry about Sonny. I got him."

Levi's tone gave Cam pause. He stopped with his hand on the truck door and looked back. Something flashed in Levi's eyes. Betrayal? No. Cam couldn't have that. Sonny's secret was precious, and one Cam had discovered by accident, but he couldn't let Levi believe that Sonny was anything less than the brilliant young man he was.

"It's not what you think."

Levi's gaze hardened. Despite the cryptic overtone, he knew exactly what Cam was talking about. "I ain't judging him, but I can't watch him destroy himself. I can't go through that again."

"It's not his fault."

"Isn't it?" Levi looked away.

Cam grasped Levi's arm, forcing him to look back. "It's *not*. He's not a coke whore, Levi. It's fucking Ritalin. He's been on it since he was twelve."

Levi stared at him, his dark gaze flickering with unanswered questions, but it was the wrong time. Cam loved Sonny and Levi probably more than he should've, but Levi was right. He'd run out of time to worry about anyone but himself.

"It's okay, Cam." Levi reached across him and shoved open the passenger door. "Everything's gonna be okay. You take care of this, and I'll take care of Sonny."

Cam paced his hospital room, his socked feet making no sound on the shiny white floor. Wade watched him from the chair at the side of the bed, his shrewd gaze tracking Cam's every move.

"Sit down, Son. You'll wear yourself out before they've even got started."

Cam ignored him. Wade's presence was comforting, but with just a few minutes to go until they came to shoot who knew what into the

IV in his hand, his nerves were getting the better of him. He stopped at the window and stared out over the hospital grounds. Wade's reaction to the cancer had been predictable—a horrified silence and then a bone-crushing hug that stole the breath from Cam's lungs. A day on the couch, a hot meal, and a good night sleep in his childhood bed had followed, but even the comfort of home and what remained of his family wasn't enough to quell the fast-rising panic in his belly.

This was it. There was no going back. In a few short hours he'd wake up literally half the man he used to be.

"Are you sure you don't want me to call your mom?"

Cam considered the question, anything to keep his mind from his condemned anatomy. He hadn't spoken to his mom for so long he couldn't recall if her presence had ever made him feel better. And what about Wade? He'd taken his wife's departure with dignity and grace, but Cam remembered the pain in his eyes as she'd driven away into the sunset, leaving her four kids and the only life they'd ever known far behind.

Screw her. "I'm fine, Dad. I don't need her."

Wade's sigh was soft, but Cam heard it like a supersonic boom. Felt it like the sledgehammer of a text message Sonny had sent him long before dawn that morning.

Get better. We love you — S

Five little words, words that meant everything and nothing, because despite it all, Cam still felt totally and utterly alone. His room had been a revolving door of doctors and nurses, waving forms for him to sign, poking him with needles, and jamming things into his ears and mouth, but the sense that someone was missing lingered, and the only thing Cam knew for sure was it wasn't his damned mother.

"Mr. Shaw?" Cam looked around. A nurse stood in the doorway, flanked by an orderly with a wheelchair. "It's time to take you to the OR."

Nausea rolled in the pit of Cam's stomach. He stared at the wheelchair and willed himself to man up and step forward, but he couldn't do it. "I don't need a wheelchair."

"It's either that or we wheel you down on a gurney."

"I can walk."

The nurse looked irritated, as though she'd had the conversation a thousand times that day already. "It's procedure."

"Let the boy walk," Wade said. "Can't do no harm."

The nurse relented and let Cam shuffle past her in his hospital gown and socks, but the orderly followed close behind, brandishing the wheelchair like a gun.

Cam drifted along the corridor in a daze, his legs like lead. His chest hurt. It took him a few steps to realize he'd stopped breathing. He sucked in a harsh breath. A choked noise escaped him. Wade touched his arm.

"Easy, Son."

The gesture, and the appearance of the imposing double door to the operating room, reminded Cam that they were moments away from being separated. Terror bubbled up in his throat. He opened his mouth to call for his dad, but the words never came.

"Cam! Cam, wait."

Cam looked over his shoulder. The hospital corridor moved in slow motion, and Sasha appeared in front of him like a dream, his hair crazy and windswept, his eyes wild.

Cam stared at him. "What are you doing here?"

Sasha took his hands and squeezed them in a grip so tight it should've hurt. "I… Fuck. I had to see you before you went in. I'm so sorry, Cam."

Cam stared. Somewhere in the back of his mind he knew they were surrounded by nurses and orderlies…even his own father, but the rest of the world faded away. "What are you sorry for?"

Sasha kissed him, lightly at first, but then harder…kissed him until Cam swayed on his feet. "For everything. I'm sorry I made you feel like shit, and I'm sorry I pushed you away so many times. Get through this, and I promise, I'll never push you away again."

CHAPTER THIRTEEN

Cam opened his eyes. It seemed like no time at all had passed since a white-masked doctor had instructed him to count backward from one hundred, but if the brutal pain in his belly was anything to go by, he'd made it through the surgery.

He swallowed, trying to make sense of the stretched tension in his groin and the numbness down his left side. His back felt stiff. He shifted to relieve the pressure and cringed. Bad move. *Fuck*, that hurt.

Someone called his name. He peeled his eyes open again and found his father's steady gaze.

"Okay, Son?" Wade squeezed his hand. "The nurse put a pain pump in your hand. Press the button if you're uncomfortable."

The instructions rang a bell. Cam vaguely remembered the surgeon explaining the self-administering morphine pump to him. At the time, he'd figured he wouldn't need it. How bad could it be?

Pretty fucking bad, as it turned out. Cam pressed the button.

His faculties returned to him one by one. Beyond the pain, he felt sleepy and sick, but the feeling faded as the fog clouding his brain lifted. "Dad?"

Wade rubbed his shoulder. "I'm here, Son. Everything's okay. The procedure went well."

Cam frowned. The words were reassuring, but it wasn't what he wanted to hear. There was a gap in his mind. Something...someone was missing, but who? Cam peeled his tongue from the roof of his mouth and tried to articulate the nameless face in his mind. "Sash?"

Nearly. It would have to do, and when Sasha appeared in his sight line, he didn't seem to mind the slurred, shortened version of his name. He squeezed Cam's other hand. "I'm here."

Cam smiled. He could feel the effects of whatever was in the pump beginning to seep into his body, and it felt *good*. Seeing Sasha grinning at Wade, like they'd known each other years rather than just a few hours, felt good too. "Where's your bike?"

"At home." Sasha chuckled and touched his cheek. "Sleep it off, dude. I'll be here when you wake up."

Cam stared at the area between his legs reflected in the mirror. "Are you sure it doesn't look weird?"

Levi sighed. He'd been Cam's first visitor that morning, with a subdued Sonny in tow, and he already looked fed up. "Stop staring at your dick. It doesn't even look that different."

"What about up close? What if you were blowing me?"

Sonny snorted from his perch on the window ledge, the first sound he'd made since he'd drifted into the room behind Levi, red-eyed and disheveled. He'd sat behind Cam on the bed for a while, combing his fingers through Cam's hair, but he'd retreated when a doctor had checked in, and he'd yet to return. "When did *Levi* last blow *you*?"

It was true. Giving Levi head was way too much fun to let him reciprocate all that often. The big man loved a good blowjob, and it was always fun to watch him unravel. "Okay, fine. Can *you* look then?" Sonny hesitated. Cam held out his hand and beckoned him forward. "Please? For me? You're the only one I can trust to tell me the truth."

"Hey." Levi looked put out.

Cam rolled his eyes. "Come on. Are you seriously telling me you weren't going to tell me everything is just fine and dandy?"

"It is. I wouldn't lie to you."

Cam wasn't convinced. Despite his enduring rep on the porn scene, Levi was a nice guy. Too nice. Sonny would give it to him straight.

Sonny slid off the window ledge. He took Cam's hand and kissed his cheek. Cam nudged him with his shoulder. Sonny was a firecracker, but he didn't seem himself today. Cam wondered if something had gone down between him and Levi. Then he wondered if Sonny was pissed at him for telling Levi about the Ritalin. But he didn't look pissed, he looked…sad. Which wasn't like Sonny at all. Sonny was vibrant and exuberant, a free spirit in every sense of the word. It bothered Cam to see him so down.

Sonny kissed Cam again and averted his gaze to Cam's groin. "Does it hurt?"

Cam glanced down. A dressing covered the three-inch incision in his groin. It hurt when he moved or stretched too far, but otherwise, the pain pills the nurses were feeding him at regular intervals were doing their job. "Just aches a bit."

"You look better than I thought you would."

Cam drummed his fingers on the mattress. He *felt* better than he'd thought he would, but he didn't give a shit about that. He wanted to know what Sonny thought of his lopsided balls. "I'm *fine*."

Sonny took the hint and stooped to take a proper look. He kept his distance at first, hesitant for reasons only he knew. Cam got impatient, grabbed the back of Sonny's head, and shoved him closer.

"Okay, okay. I'm looking." Sonny laughed and wriggled out of Cam's grip. "Hey, that doesn't look so bad. I thought you'd look mutilated."

"Not helping, Son."

Sonny huffed. Cam felt his breath on his thigh. "I'm being positive. It looks fine, Cam. I mean, I can tell something's missing, but it doesn't look weird."

"Even up close?"

"I'd blow you."

Cam swiveled his gaze to Levi. "What about you?"

Levi rolled his eyes. "I would as it is now."

Sonny glanced over his shoulder. "What's that supposed to mean?"

Cam reached behind him and snagged the plastic implant he'd shown Levi while Sonny had been in the bathroom. Cam had opted not to have it inserted immediately, and judging by Levi and Sonny's collective reaction, he'd made the right decision.

"A fake nut?" Sonny batted the bouncy rubber away. "Fuck that. You don't need that. Levi, come see. He doesn't need a fake one, right?"

"That's what I just said." Levi grumbled but dropped down beside Sonny all the same. "It doesn't even look like something's missing. It just looks…smaller."

"Smaller?" Cam let his dick go so it hung over his balls. "What about now?"

Sonny and Levi both looked closer. Of course Sasha chose that moment to open the door. "Cam? Oh. Shit. Sorry."

Cam met Sasha's liquid gaze and forgot all about his friends at his knees. "Hey."

"Hey, yourself." Sasha ventured farther into the room. "Is this a private party, or can anyone play?"

"Depends," Sonny quipped from the floor. "Do you have lopsided balls? We're doing an in-depth analysis here."

Cam shot Sonny a look. He hadn't told anyone about Sasha's history. Sasha had been by his side since he'd come around from the surgery two days ago, flanked by Wade, but they'd yet to talk about anything other than Cam's immediate state of health. Cam had been too groggy and distracted by the line of painful stitches in his belly.

But he felt better today, bright and alert. Alert enough to worry about scaring Sasha away before they'd had a chance to reconnect. Cam stared at Sasha and felt his stress levels rise. He didn't have it in him to watch Sasha walk away again.

Sasha held his gaze for a long moment; then he undid his fly and dropped his jeans. "See for yourself."

Cam's mouth fell open.

Sasha shrugged, unfazed. "What? You think I don't like getting naked?"

Cam had no answer, both shocked and caught in a haze of intense curiosity. "Come closer."

Sasha took a few steps forward and lifted his T-shirt so Cam could see what remained of his balls. "See? Looks just fine, right?"

Cam stared, transfixed. Below Sasha's taut, tanned abdomen lay an image of what his own body would look like when the scars and swollen flesh had faded away.

Sonny held out his hand and helped Cam down from the bed. "Stand together. Let me look properly."

Cam wondered if now was the best time to introduce them all, but he was distracted by Sasha's cock. Though soft and limp, it was thick and long, the kind of cock every porn star wished they had.

Sonny stooped again and whistled. "Who needs balls, huh? You both look good enough to eat."

Levi rolled his eyes. "Okay, now we all know that, it's time we weren't here. Sonny, come on. I gotta get to the garage."

For a moment, nobody moved. Then Sasha pulled his jeans up, fastened them, and held out his hand to Sonny. "Hey. I'm Sasha."

Sonny took Sasha's hand and grinned. "I kinda figured. Levi told me how hot you were."

Cam let his hospital gown drop and cut his gaze to Levi. "How did you know Sasha was hot?"

"We met yesterday. I was on my way out as Sasha was coming in."

"You were here yesterday?" Cam frowned. He didn't remember much of the day before. He'd spent most of it asleep. He remembered Kay talking his ear off about some meditation class he just *had* to take, and Sasha… Cam could remember the low rumble of his voice, but Levi? Nope. Cam couldn't recall seeing him at all.

Levi said nothing, but his eyes glittered, betraying his mirth over something Cam didn't understand.

Sonny came to Cam and kissed his cheek. "I'll come by tomorrow. Feel better, okay?"

Cam swallowed a lump in his throat. Sonny looked so sad he couldn't stand it, but Sonny ducked out of the room before he could speak.

Levi started to follow, but Cam grabbed his arm. "What's going on with you two?"

Levi sighed and steadied Cam. "We're going to spend some time apart…I think. Maybe. It's complicated."

"What?" Cam felt his stomach turn over. "I didn't tell you his private shit so you could ditch him. Come on, man."

"I'm not ditching him. I would never do that. I love…" Levi cast a glance at Sasha, who was pretending not to listen. "Fuck. Look, Sonny needs to figure out what he wants. I can't *make* him better. He's got to want it, Cam, and I don't know if he does."

Levi was wrong. Sonny did want to get better; he just didn't know how. No one did. Sonny had been popping Ritalin since he was a kid, and that was only the start of it. Manic highs and crippling lows, Sonny was probably sicker than Cam was, and he needed help Cam couldn't give him. "Levi, help him."

"I will." Levi drew Cam into a hug and pressed his face into Cam's neck. "But he's got to want it."

Levi departed, leaving Cam alone with Sasha. Sasha was silent as Cam hoisted himself back onto the bed. Cam eyed him, wondering how he felt seeing Cam so casually tactile with his friends. Levi didn't seem to mind the closeness Cam and Sonny shared, but it was different for him. Porn had changed his perception of relationships. Sasha had never had that, and though they'd yet to define their relationship, Cam knew they had much to talk about.

Sasha eased himself carefully between Cam's legs. "Close your mouth, Cam. You look like you're catching flies."

"Huh?"

"You look shell-shocked. What's up?"

There were so many answers to that question. Cam went with the least painful. "How come you showed Sonny your balls, but you didn't show me?"

Sasha's eyes widened, and then he laughed a real, deep belly laugh that filled the room and overpowered some of Cam's worries. "I never meant to, it just kinda happened, but you should know, I'm not quite the prude I've made myself out to be."

Cam raised an eyebrow, intrigued despite the pain in his groin. "What do you mean?"

Sasha sighed. "I don't want to get into the whole sex thing right now. That'll come for us, if it's meant to, but I don't want you to ever think what happened to you…to both of us, is something to be embarrassed about."

"I don't think that."

"Yeah, you do, and I reckon I haven't done much to help you with that." Sasha fiddled with Cam's hospital gown. "I was embarrassed… Fuck, I was mortified when you touched me that time in the club, and then I was so pissed off when I realized it was going to happen to you."

Sasha stopped. Cam wanted to say something…anything to comfort him, but he somehow knew Sasha had more to say.

"I'd just about gotten over it when you came to my place. I figured we'd talk and find a way to make it right, for both of us, but then I saw you... Fuck, Cam, I knew you were losing it. If we'd hooked up that day, you'd have wound up hating me for it, or at least regretted it. I couldn't bear that."

Cam shook his head. His heart ached, but he didn't believe it, not for a second. "I could never hate you."

Sasha smiled. "That's sweet, but don't underestimate what this demon can do to you. We'll talk about us, I promise, but for now, just know I'm not going anywhere, okay? I'm here, in whatever capacity you want me, for as long as you'll have me."

"And we'll talk about the sex? Soon, yeah?" Damn it. Cam wanted to say something profound, but it seemed his narcotic-addled brain had other ideas.

Sasha laughed and kissed Cam's forehead. "Soon. I promise. Now forget about it for a while, okay? Did the doctor come by yet?"

"What?" Cam felt himself return to earth with a clunk. "Oh, yeah. He came before Levi and Sonny. He said I can go home later today."

"What else did he say?"

Cam heard the question Sasha didn't ask. He wanted to know the results of the path tests on the tumor. "Same thing he said before the surgery. It's cancer."

Cam said the words with little emotion. The confirmation of his initial diagnosis didn't mean much to him, because he hadn't expected anything else. The plan was the same as it had always been. Cut the bastard out and nuke his body with radiation. What else was there to say?

Sasha rubbed Cam's shoulder and combed his fingers through Cam's hair with his other hand. Cam closed his eyes. Two days in bed had left his hair a mess—tangled and wild. Sonny had picked his way through some of it, but somehow Sasha found a few errant knots.

Cam sighed and felt himself relax. Sasha's touch felt good. *Too* good. Cam knew it would be all too easy to float away on it and ignore the nagging sensation in his brain that he had no right to enjoy Sasha's easy affection, the affection that, ever since he'd come around from the surgery, had slipped into his life like it had always been there. He opened his eyes and caught Sasha's wandering hands. "I need to tell you something."

Sasha regarded him with his warm, open gaze. "Okay. Let's hear it."

Cam chewed the inside of his mouth, unsure of where to start. "You know who Levi and Sonny are, right? You know I work with them?"

Sasha nodded. "I've, um, seen them around."

"Well, I kinda…the other night…" Cam lost his words. How did he explain what had gone down between the three of them? How did he explain how much he'd needed the warmth and love of his friends without sounding like a needy whore?

Sasha's chuckle caught him off guard. "You're not gonna tell me all about Sonny's fuck-hot blowjob again, are you?"

"Huh?"

Sasha smirked. "Cam, you told me about Levi and Sonny two days ago. Yes, I know you fooled around with them and, no, I don't think you're a whore."

"What? When…what, exactly, did I tell you?"

Cam was officially lost. The last few days were a little fuzzy, but he'd remember something like that, right?

Apparently not, much to Sasha's obvious amusement. "You were babbling about it when you came out of surgery. Think it was the drugs they gave you."

"What did I say?"

"Not much. Just that you'd had some kinda three-way, and that you were thinking of me the whole time."

Cam winced. "Did I really say that?"

Sasha held his gaze for a moment, then broke out a grin that made Cam feel twenty pounds lighter. "Guess you'll never know, huh?"

Cam laughed, but then he sobered. "I wasn't rambling, you

know. It's true. Levi and Sonny are my friends, but things sometimes get…"

Damn it. Cam lost his train of thought again, but it didn't seem to matter.

Sasha squeezed his hands. "I get it, okay? At least, I think I do. I'm not gonna lie. I've slept with, like, four people, and I'm not friends with anyone the way you're friends with them, but I *know* you don't look at them the same way you do me."

"You do?"

"Yeah. Listen, I don't know how dealing with this…" Sasha gestured around the hospital room. "How any of it is going to affect you, but for me, confronting my mortality taught me to look beyond the obvious. I forgot that for a while when we first met, but I'm back on it now."

Cam rubbed his face as a wave of postsurgical fatigue washed over him. "I love them. They're my best friends."

Sasha eased Cam into a careful hug. "I know, and I can see how much they love each other too. I'd be mad if I thought that was wrong. Besides, you were right about Levi. He's pretty sharp, huh?"

Cam had almost forgotten the long-ago conversation at the sushi bar. "Yeah, he is. He's good for Sonny. Sonny's a little…"

"Wild?"

Cam hummed his agreement. It was hard to concentrate with Sasha kneading the back of his neck.

"Cam, you still with me?"

"Just about." Cam raised his head.

Sasha smiled back at him a moment before he fell serious again. "I don't want you to worry about the porn thing. If I had a problem with it, I wouldn't be here. I'm not saying I want to have a gang bang with your friends, but I know who you are, and I like it. I like *you*, okay?"

"Sonny thinks I look for answers in sex."

"Then use this as a clean slate. Take the bones of who you are and make it better."

"You don't hate me?"

"For what? Seeking comfort from your friends when I pushed you away? No, of course I don't. I know you come from a different way of life, and I'm glad they were there for you."

Cam couldn't quite believe it was as simple as that, but for now, he let it go. He was tired, but he felt antsy and wanted more than anything to escape the sterile, white walls of the hospital.

"So…" Sasha let the word hang. "Now we've figured out we're both on the same page, I want to ask you something too."

Cam raised an eyebrow, curious. "Oh, yeah?"

"Yeah. I was talking to your dad, and he said he's gotta work a lot next week. With your kid brothers and all, I reckon he's going to have his hands full."

Cam nodded. That was nothing new. Kay helped out where she could, but Wade spent most of his time running in circles between sports clubs and the grocery store. "So?"

"*So* how would you feel about staying with me for a few days? You can have my bed, and I can take care of you while you recuperate."

"Recuperate?"

Sasha flicked his arm. "Yeah. Cam, you just had surgery. You need to rest and take it easy."

Cam considered Sasha's offer. He didn't want Wade running around after him, and the thought of going home to his empty apartment was depressing, but he had one issue with Sasha's offer. He used his legs to hook Sasha closer and wrapped his arms around Sasha's waist. "Dude, the only way I'm sleeping in your bed is if you're right there next to me. What do you say?"

Sasha grinned and kissed Cam's forehead. "I say…hell, yeah."

CHAPTER FOURTEEN

Cam took his place at the end of the on-set couch. Sonny dropped down beside him and curled into his side.

Sonny trembled. The shudder was subtle, but Cam felt it ripple through him. He put his arm around Sonny and kissed the top of his head. Sonny's answering sigh was shaky and soft, but he sat up again before Cam could press him. "This feels weird. Something's up."

Cam glanced around the studio and was inclined to agree. He and Sonny were on-set at Blue Boy, like they'd been so many times before, but the scene that surrounded them wasn't anything like the usual preparations for a shoot. There were no cameras or specialist lights, just every staff member Blue Boy employed, cast and crew, sitting around and waiting…but for what? Cam had no idea. All he knew was Sherry, the studio's receptionist, had left a message on his voice mail requesting his presence for a full staff meeting, and though porn was the last thing on Cam's mind, the prospect of a studio full of witnesses seemed the ideal time to face Jon for the first time since Cam had trashed his computer. All he needed now was for Jon to drag his sorry ass out of his office.

Sonny nudged him. "How are you feeling?"

Cam shrugged. No one was supposed to know about the surgery, but a few models had noticed he wasn't quite himself. "I feel good, man. Can't even feel it anymore."

"Really?"

"Really." Cam understood Sonny's skepticism, but it was true. It had been a month or so since the surgery, and all things considered, he felt pretty good. His planned short stay at Sasha's poolside bungalow had turned into an extended vacation, and aside from some irritating numbness in his lower belly, he felt healthier than he had in years.

Perhaps it was the lack of beer and the freakishly healthy diet Sasha was feeding him. Who cared? Not him. He felt great, and that was enough for him.

Sasha. Cam grinned as his mind got away from him. Despite the inconvenience of having surgery, the past few months had been...enlightening. Getting to know Sasha was a lot of fun, and the tentative affection they'd begun in the hospital had become something more. Cam couldn't imagine his life without Sasha now. Didn't want to. The hours they'd spent talking, kissing, and just being together were branded on him in a way he'd never imagined. The only thing missing was...

Jon's office door opened. Cam tensed, and all thoughts of finally getting Sasha naked evaporated. He squared his shoulders and prepared to do battle, but his words died in his throat when he realized he was glaring not at Jon, but at a total stranger. A freakin' *huge* stranger.

The tall, bear-shaped man was followed out of the office by another man, smaller in stature but with a similar build. Both in their late thirties, at first glance, the men looked like brothers, though looking closer and absorbing the heated stare that passed between them, Cam could tell they were lovers. *Real* lovers.

The men crossed the studio and came to a stop where most of the cast and crew had gathered in a loose semicircle. A hush fell over the group, and the taller man smiled, showing a set of perfect white teeth and a grin that rivaled Sasha's in warmth. "Afternoon, folks. Thanks for joining us at such short notice. We'll keep this brief. I'm sure you've got lives to get back to."

The smaller man stepped forward. "I'm Jude Regan. This is my partner, Mac, and we are the new owners and directors of Blue Boy Enterprises. As of last night, the studio, and all businesses attached to it belong to us."

There was a collective, stunned silence. Cam felt the numbness in his belly spread throughout his body. Jon had sold Blue Boy? That didn't make any sense. The studio was his life's work, his passion. *His obsession.* Why would he sell it?

"What about Silver?" Sonny called out. He looked relieved, and Cam could understand that. Levi hated Jon. Sonny's life would be much easier without him on the scene.

"Yep. Silver too." Jude nodded to Mac, who held up a stack of paperwork. "Over the next few days we will be meeting with each of you individually and reviewing your contracts. Dancers, models, backroom staff, we'll be talking to you all."

An anxious hum rippled through the studio. Jude signaled for quiet. "Easy, folks. No one's getting fired. We just feel this is a good time for all of us to take stock and figure out what direction we're going, to move forward. You have a strong base here, but we believe we can make it better. Move beyond the commercial markets and create something special."

"In the same vein," Mac said, "this is also a chance for you to renegotiate contracts you're not happy with, or sever them completely if you feel you've outgrown the industry. It happens, and we're not here to fuck anyone over."

"What about outstanding payments?"

Cam glanced at Caleb and rolled his eyes. That dude was all about the money.

Jude said, "All payments outstanding will be honored. Silver will continue to operate as normal, but for the next few weeks Blue Boy Studio will be temporarily shut down while we figure things out behind the scenes. I know you all probably have questions, but rather than keeping you all here for hours, save them for your one-on-ones."

It seemed to be a dismissal, but nobody moved. Cam took a deep breath. Jon's disappearance was a weight off his mind, but he couldn't imagine Blue Boy without him. The guy was a douche, but he hadn't always been that way. In the beginning, he'd taught Cam how to survive in a brutal industry.

Sonny squeezed his thigh. "You okay?"

"Hmm?"

"You're not upset about Jon leaving, are you?"

Cam frowned. Was he? No, that wasn't it. "I don't think so."

Sonny raised an eyebrow, considering him, and Cam knew he was running through the bank of psychology theory he had stacked up in his big-ass brain. "Ah, I get it. It's fucked up your plan. You were going to quit, weren't you? Now you're not sure if you want to."

Cam sighed. Sonny might've been on to something, but before they could hash it out, Jude called Cam's name. It seemed they'd decided that Cam was at the top of their list.

"I'm on tomorrow's list," Sonny said. "Do you want me to wait for you?"

Cam got to his feet. Sonny had been miserable for weeks, and Levi didn't seem to be faring much better. Cam had tried to get them to talk about whatever had gone wrong between them, but it was like banging his head against a brick wall. They'd both been frequent visitors at Sasha's place, but never together, and that made Cam's heart ache. He didn't know what Levi was hoping to achieve, but he knew for sure it wasn't doing Sonny any good at all. "Nah. I got this. Go home and get some sleep. I'll call you later, okay?"

He left Sonny on the couch and made his way to the office. He hadn't set foot in there since Jon had tried to fuck him over the desk, but when he got inside, he saw that overnight, the office had been stripped of anything that reminded him of Jon. It was like a different world.

"Have a seat." Mac shut the door and leaned against the wall.

Cam eyed them both and dropped into the nearest chair. He felt like he recognized Jude, though he couldn't say where from. "Any reason you hauled me in first?"

"Not really." Jude pulled what Cam assumed was his contract from a desk drawer. "You are one of the longest-serving models, though. You seemed a good place to start." Jude flipped through the paperwork. "You've not been around much the last few months. Thinking about moving on?"

Cam shrugged. "Maybe, but that's not why I haven't been around."

Jude gestured for him to elaborate. Cam analyzed him a moment, then thought, fuck it. What did he have to lose? He had nothing to hide, and keeping secrets had proved a toxic game. "There's a few reasons I haven't been around lately," he said. "And they're all pretty fucked up."

"Go on," Mac said from his position by the door. "We heard a rumor you and Jon were together. What happened? Did you break up?"

"Something like that. We've been on bad terms for a while. He made some videos of me without my consent."

Jude exchanged an inscrutable look with Mac. "That's not cool, but you should know Jon's gone for good. Last we heard he was headed East Coast way to start fresh. That's not it, though, is it? What else is bugging you?"

Cam wondered when he'd become so easy to read. "I was diagnosed with testicular cancer a few months ago. I've had surgery, but I've got a course of treatment coming up. I'm going to be out of action for a while, if I come back at all."

There. He'd said it, and it felt…refreshing.

Jude made a note in his file. "That's rough, and we're sorry to hear that. I want you to know your contract and all its benefits will remain valid until you say otherwise, whether you work for us again or not."

"Thanks. I appreciate that." Cam would be lying if he said he hadn't worried about how leaving Blue Boy would affect his insurance status. He'd even considered filming a few scenes between treatments to keep his contract intact.

At least he had until Sasha.

Sasha, Sasha, Sasha…

Mac said something. Cam blinked. "Huh?"

Jude grinned. "He said, we've just bought a new house in Venice Beach. When we're settled you should come over for dinner, bring your guy."

"How do you know I have a guy?"

"Because I know that look." Jude shot another loaded glance at Mac. "Seems like you've got a lot of figuring out to do, but whatever happens, even if you don't feel up to filming again, there's probably a role for you behind the scenes. You've been here a long time. New models need someone like you to guide them. Someone who's not signing their paychecks."

"It's something to think on, Cam," Mac said. "You're a popular model, and we want you to stay, but we understand that's not a decision you can make right now. Take as much time as you need, and come and see us again when you're ready."

Cam nodded and took it as his dismissal, but he didn't get up. For some reason, he couldn't stop staring at Jude.

Jude cocked his head to the side and gave him a boyish grin. "Something else you want to talk about?"

"Where are you from? I feel like I've seen you before."

Mac snorted. Jude rolled his eyes and opened a desk drawer. "Maybe you have."

He tossed a DVD case on the table. Cam picked it up, studied the cover, and staring back at him he found a younger version of Jude, tied up in leather and chains. Wow. The dude was *hot*, and Cam recognized the name—Rocco Vain. Fuck, Jude was a living legend, in the porn world, at least. "You were a model?"

"For a long time. I've been out of the game for a while; we both have." Jude glanced at Mac. "But we're back now, and we're going to do it right, Cam. Whatever happens, we'll take care of you."

Cam walked out of the studio feeling twenty pounds lighter, and in a good way. Jude and Mac seemed like decent guys. He'd felt comfortable spilling his guts to them, and the idea of putting off a decision about porn was appealing. His head was all over the place, and he wasn't entirely convinced by Sasha's claim that he was cool with dating a porn star.

He climbed into Sasha's truck and drove back to the bungalow. Sasha was tinkering with his BMX on a plastic table by the pool, his hands smeared with oil. He was a sight for sore eyes, but Cam blurted out the events of the meeting before he had a chance to brood on it.

Sasha showed no emotion at the news of Blue Boy's management transition, and Cam wasn't surprised. Sasha didn't know all the gory details, but he'd made his views on Jon clear.

"I don't want to know anything about that manipulative asshole," he'd said. *"There's some shit I'm better off not knowing."*

"What are you going to do?" Sasha wiped his hands on his T-shirt. "Do you want to go back?"

"I don't know. I need to get through my treatment first. I haven't thought much beyond that."

"But?"

Cam shrugged. "I *like* porn. To me, it doesn't feel dirty or wrong, and it's something I'm good at. Even if I don't film again, I can't imagine not having it in my life. Does that sound weird?"

"No." Sasha paused, and Cam could tell he was choosing his words with care. "And I don't think you should worry about what it sounds like. The people who matter have your back."

Cam thought of his family, his friends, and the man who was fast becoming the love of his life. "I know that."

"So don't worry about it. Get better, and after, if you want to go back and finish what you started, you can fret over it then."

"I'm not fretting."

"Oh, yeah?" Sasha pulled Cam close and rubbed the pad of his thumb on Cam's forehead. "Stop frowning then. Makes you look old."

Cam's retort was swallowed by a fuck-hot kiss, the kind of kiss that went on and on, until he forgot the rest of the world existed. The kind of kiss that should've led to more but didn't because Sasha pulled away.

"We need to talk about something else." Sasha looked pensive. "I think we've got some shit we need to work out."

Cam steeled himself. He'd noticed Sasha had been quiet the past few days, and for once, he figured he knew why. Sex. It had to be. They'd been sleeping side by side for weeks but hadn't ventured beyond hours and hours of kissing like teenagers. It had been the longest Cam had been without sex in years, and though he'd fast learned there was more to life than fucking, he knew they'd also reached a tipping point. Something had to give, and he'd made up his mind long ago that it was going to be him. "I know what you're going to say."

Sasha raised an eyebrow. "Do you?"

Cam let his arms drop from around Sasha's waist and pointed to the swinging chair. "I reckon so. Come sit with me?"

Sasha let Cam tug him to the seat. They sat close together, not touching, but close enough that Cam could feel the intoxicating warmth of Sasha's solid body. "It's about the logistics, right?"

"Logistics?" Sasha looked puzzled before he caught on. "Um, yeah. Something like that. Cam, I've *seen* you. I know you don't bottom."

Do you? "So what were you thinking when you came looking for me in the hospital? That we just wouldn't have sex?"

Sasha averted his gaze. He was an open kind of guy, but talking about sex didn't come as easy to him as it did to Cam. "I guess I figured I'd…well, I decided I'd bottom…for you, if that's what you wanted."

"For me?"

"Yeah. I kinda woke up that morning and knew I'd do *anything* for you."

Cam swallowed, feeling the heated sting of tears in his eyes. "What if I said you didn't have to? That there was another way?"

"Like what?"

"Just because you've never seen me bottom on-screen doesn't mean I don't do it. You said it yourself: there's more to me than porn."

"I knew *that*, Cam, but, man, really? You really bottom?"

Sasha couldn't hide the cautious excitement in his face, and it warmed Cam's heart. "Yeah, really. I haven't done it a lot, and I'm pretty sure I've never done it right, but I want to do it with you. When I picture us together, it's what I see."

"Wow." Sasha seemed stunned. "I never thought of that. I mean, I did, but I figured it was just a fantasy."

Cam grinned. "Yeah, well. Sometimes fantasies come true."

"Oh, God." Sasha groaned. "Don't say shit like that to me. I'll be dragging you inside before you can blink."

Cam pulled off his shirt in a swift, practiced motion. "What are you waiting for?"

CHAPTER FIFTEEN

Cam let Sasha push him onto the bed. He was a little surprised they'd made it that far. Turned out Sasha knew what he wanted and wasn't afraid to take it. He was careful of the healed incision on Cam's belly, but that aside, all bets were off.

Clothes littered the hardwood floor of the bungalow. Cam's lips burned with the heat of Sasha's bruising kiss. His heart was beating out of his chest, and lower…*lower* his cock throbbed with an aching need he'd feared was gone forever.

He pushed at the waistband of Sasha's shorts. He'd felt the outline of Sasha's dick and seen it soft and limp in the hospital, but he'd imagined the sight of Sasha naked and hard over and over.

He couldn't wait any longer.

Sasha helped Cam tug his shorts over his hips. Cam kicked them away. Sasha's cock stood out, long and proud, and Cam was captivated. He had mixed feelings about the loss of his own nut, but with Sasha… Man, there was *nothing* missing there. He licked his dry lips and gripped Sasha's muscled thighs, savoring the strong legs he'd spent so long dreaming about. Whatever was going down between them, one thing wasn't in doubt. He needed Sasha's cock in his mouth.

He lay on his back, and Sasha straddled his chest. He took Sasha in his mouth, and there was something magical about Sasha's reaction as Cam opened his throat for him. Sasha gasped. His chest reddened, and sweat beaded his brow. Cam swallowed. Sasha's legs quivered, and he dug his fingers into Cam's chest.

Cam went to town on Sasha, guiding him with his hands on his hips, letting his tongue explore every inch of the man who'd become his rock. He let his hands wander, tracing Sasha's ball and trailing lower. He rubbed the rough patch of skin behind Sasha's sac and wondered…

He pulled off Sasha for air. "Have you ever?"

The question was vague and unfinished, but Sasha interpreted the meaning. He looked down at Cam with his trademark steady gaze. "Nope. I don't mind a finger or two, but never a dick. Never found the right one."

Cam tapped Sasha's entrance with the pad of his finger. Part of him wanted to plunge inside, show Sasha what he was missing, but a louder part of him knew it wasn't the right time for that. They both needed something…something safe and warm, and nothing was going to come between them.

Not today.

He swallowed Sasha whole again. Sasha moaned and shivered, and Cam drank it all in, absorbing it and filing it away in the huge cavern Sasha had carved out for himself in Cam's heart. The noises he made rattled Cam's bones, and before long, Cam was reaching for his own cock, needy and desperate.

Sasha caught the movement and batted Cam's hand away. "Uh-uh. That's mine."

Cam grinned and released Sasha's cock from his mouth. He'd put Sasha right on the edge, and knew he could make him come with a flick of his tongue, but as appealing as that was, he needed something more.

Sasha bent and kissed him before he moved down the bed, pausing to kiss Cam's surgical scar.

Cam watched, enthralled, as Sasha played his own game with Cam's dick, teasing, licking, blowing, but never taking it into his mouth. Cam writhed, enjoying the torture in a masochistic kind of way. In his mind, willing it to be over, but pleading out loud for Sasha to never, ever stop.

"Lift your leg."

Cam thrashed his head from side to side and raised his leg, expecting the probe of Sasha's fingers or the sweep of his tongue. He was sorely unprepared for the sensation of his remaining ball being sucked into Sasha's mouth. He arched his back and shuddered, twisting the sheets in his clenched fists. "Fuck!"

Sasha hummed low in his throat and then released Cam. He kissed his way up Cam's body until they were face-to-face again. "They never told you that, huh? That what you've got left is sensitive as fuck?"

Cam panted, squirming as heat rushed through his veins. "*You coulda told me.*"

"I know." Sasha placed his hands either side of Cam's head and nipped his bottom lip. "But where's the fun in that?"

Sasha ground his hips in a slow circle. His thick cock dug into Cam. Cam raised his other leg and relaxed his pelvis, straining for friction where he needed it most. Sasha's body felt so good pressed against him. Better than good. Better than he'd ever dared imagine.

He wound his arms around Sasha's neck and pulled him down for a kiss, grinding them together, desperate for more. Sasha picked up the pace and thrust against Cam with a force that made them both groan.

Sasha reached over to the nightstand and retrieved condoms and lube. Cam's pulse quickened, and his muscles clenched. Anticipation rushed through him. This was really happening, and he couldn't fucking wait.

"How do you want me?" Sasha waved the lube in Cam's face. "You said you've seen this in your head. What did you see?"

Cam wriggled out from beneath Sasha and rolled over. They'd landed sideways on the bed, and he could see the shimmering surface of the pool. "I want you to fuck me like this."

Sasha made a sound Cam hoped was a grunt of approval. Either way, a shot of excitement ran through him as Sasha nudged Cam's legs farther apart with his knees. The click of the lube bottle pierced the air. Sasha slid one finger into Cam, then two, following the natural cues of his body.

Cam gasped and ground himself into the mattress. The pressure niggled the scar on his stomach, but the discomfort was worth the bright lightning bolts of pleasure brewing inside him. "Fuck, yeah."

Sasha twisted his fingers, searching out the gland that made Cam's toes curl, but he touched it only once before he withdrew, and Cam heard the rustle and tear of the condom wrapper.

The wait seemed endless, but then it seemed that no time at all had passed before Sasha was sliding his cock between the firm muscles of Cam's ass. He teased Cam a moment, circling his entrance but not applying much pressure.

Cam growled his frustration and raised his hips. "Goddamn you. Just do it."

Sasha laughed, but he cut off as the blunt head of his cock breached Cam's body.

The burn and stretch was incredible. Cam sucked in a breath, and his eyes watered. He'd done this many times over, but never sober, and Sasha was a bigger man than Jon, in *every* way. He bit down on his lip and let out a shaky moan.

Sasha stopped and rubbed the small of Cam's back. "Okay?"

"Yeah." Cam panted out some harsh breaths. "Keep going."

Sasha eased himself all the way inside Cam. When he could go no farther, he stilled, letting Cam adjust and absorb the sensation of being filled.

Cam's eyes rolled. The pressure seeped into him, and he felt heat flush his skin. He buried his face in his arms and raised his ass, circling his hips and pushing back on Sasha's cock. Sasha held still while he did it again, and again, until he found the angle and depth that made his vision blur and his limbs feel weak.

Sasha caught his cue. He moved with care, meeting Cam halfway until he found the rhythm and took over, rocking into Cam in a motion as smooth as the tantalizing skin on his back.

Cam groaned, long and low. "So fucking good."

"Yeah?" Sasha picked up the pace and leaned over Cam, wrapping his body around him like he'd never let go. "What about this?"

Sasha claimed Cam's mouth in a bruising kiss. The distraction allowed him to snake a hand between them and grasp Cam's dick. He jerked it slowly, contrasting with the punishing slam of his hips.

Coherent speech abandoned Cam. Sasha was playing him like they'd been lovers for years, and every nerve in his body tingled, laced with a dizzying pleasure he could hardly stand. He gripped the edge of the mattress, fighting to keep his body steady. "You know…you'd make a fuck-awesome porn star, right?"

Sasha responded by releasing Cam's cock and pressing his sweat-slick palm over Cam's mouth. "Yeah? Well, you just think on that. Think about me fucking you in front of a camera, with your friends watching us."

Cam's toes curled, and there was no denying the thrill that ran through him. Sasha wasn't serious, he couldn't be, but the thought alone was enough to make him cry out. The notion spread, from his lust-crazed mind to his heart, and in that moment, he knew that if he ever had sex on-screen again, it would be with Sasha. He shrugged away from Sasha's hand. "Tease."

Sasha chuckled, but then the vibe between them shifted. Deepened. Sasha slowed his brutal pace and wrapped his arms around

Cam, holding him tight and keeping them both balanced as Cam faltered. The unmistakable scent of sex hung in the air, punctuated by the protesting slide of the bed on the hardwood floor. Cam felt liquid. He gave himself up to Sasha and let the slow grind of their bodies moving together take over his whole being. He hid his face in the crook of his arm again and took himself in hand, chasing the building pleasure he craved so much.

Sasha covered him with his whole body, murmured words of encouragement, and fused his lips to Cam's neck. Cam wanted to weep as he realized that this was what he'd been missing…searching for all along—the undeniable sensation of shaking in a man's arms, of being held like he was that man's whole world. Sasha's world.

Orgasm hit. Every part of his body tightened with painful pleasure, and he came with a guttural cry. Wet warmth spilled over his fingers. He fell slack in Sasha's arms and moaned again. Sasha's rhythm became stuttered and sharp, and with one last, stabbing thrust he stilled and groaned low and deep in Cam's ear. Heat pooled where they were joined. Cam whimpered. The sensation was almost too much. He convulsed, racked with whole-body shudders, and collapsed on himself as Sasha let him go.

Sasha lay over him, quiet and still, pressing soft kisses between Cam's shoulder blades until Cam felt able to raise his head and look around. Sasha met his gaze with a gentle grin. "Okay?"

Cam nodded. "Yeah. That was…fuck."

He had no other words. His tongue felt loose and swollen, and his mind too hazy to think. He felt inside out. Claimed, desired, and…loved. He felt whole.

Sasha kissed him once more before he rose, fetched a towel, and cleaned them both up. Then he pulled back the comforter and coaxed Cam into the bed. Cam felt boneless as he crawled under the covers and collapsed in a heap. Jon had pushed him physically in the bedroom, but he'd never felt connected to him. Something was always missing. Being with Sasha was beyond different. It was mind-blowing, and he felt *wrecked*.

Sasha stretched out beside him, pushed Cam's sweat-damp hair away from his face, and kissed his forehead. "Wow. I didn't think I'd ever see you like that."

Cam trembled; he couldn't help it. He felt like his body was not his own. "Like what?"

"So…" Sasha seemed to search for the right word. "Involved, maybe? On-screen, you all seem kinda cold. I guess I figured you'd done it all before."

Cam took a moment to gather himself. A phrase came to him, and he allowed himself a wry grin. "It's not the same. That's work, even if it's one of my friends. This is real sex."

"Real sex, huh?" Sasha shifted onto his back and pulled Cam against him. "I can live with that."

Cam closed his eyes and sank into the warmth of Sasha's chuckle and the comforting weight of his arms around him. He'd been afraid since the bright summer day his mom walked out of his life, but now, despite the looming prospect of treatment and the uncertainties that came with it, with Sasha he felt like he could take on the world.

Take on the world and win.

THE END

TITLES BY GARRETT LEIGH

The BLUE BOY Series
Bullet
Bones
Bold
Coming soon: Brave

Also by **GARRETT LEIGH**
Slide
Marked
Rare
Freed

Misfits
Strays

My Mate Jack
Lucky Man

Only Love
Heart
Between Ghosts
Rented Heart

GARRETT LEIGH

NOTE: The best way to keep up to date with the day-to-day chaos that is Garrett is to join her Facebook fan group, Garrett's Den... facebook.com/groups/garrettsden

Garrett Leigh is an award-winning British writer and book designer, currently working for Dreamspinner Press, Loose Id, Riptide Publishing, and Fox Love Press. Her debut novel, Slide, won Best Bisexual Debut at the 2014 Rainbow Book Awards, and her polyamorous novel, Misfits was a finalist in the 2016 LAMBDA awards.

When not writing, Garrett can generally be found procrastinating on Twitter, cooking up a storm, or sitting on her behind doing as little as possible, all the while shouting at her menagerie of children and animals and attempting to tame her unruly and wonderful FOX.

Garrett is also an award winning cover artist, taking the silver medal at the Benjamin Franklin Book Awards in 2016. She designs for various publishing houses and independent authors at blackjazzdesign.com, and co-owns the specialist stock site moonstockphotography.com

Links to reach Garrett:
Main Web page: garrettleigh.com
Twitter: twitter.com/Garrett_Leigh
Facebook: facebook.com/garrettleighbooks
Instagram: instagram.com/garrett_leigh
Cover Art: blackjazzdesign.com